A Sinner's Virtue

De Bellis Crime Family
Book 3

kylie Kent

Club Omerta

Are you a part of the Club?

Don't want to wait for the next book to be released to the public?
Come and Club Omerta for an all access pass!

This includes:
- daily chapter reveals,
- first to see - everything, covers, teasers, blurbs
- Advanced reader copies of every book
- Bonus scenes from the characters you love!
- Video chats with me (Kylie Kent)
- and so much more

Click the link to be inducted to the club!!!

CLUB OMERTA

Cover Illustration by Cover Kate Farlow – Y'all That Graphic

Edited By
Kat Pagan

Foreword

Content warning. This is a dark mafia romance. Please read with caution. Topics found within these pages include but are not limited to: sexual assault, graphic violence, blood, death, and adult language.

Chapter One

The smell of smoke fills the room, the lights dim and the music loud. Every man's fantasy can be found within these four walls. We make sure there's a flavour to satisfy every kind of appetite. Our dancers come in all shapes and sizes.

Tonight, I can't help but be disinterested in the

product. I glance at my brothers. Gio and Santo are both showing the same indifference.

Gio, the eldest out of the five of us, sports that look permanently. I wouldn't be surprised if he came straight out of the womb with a scowl on his face. My big brother has spent his entire life being groomed to take over the family business, just as soon as our old man fucking dies. Which, in my humble opinion, couldn't come soon enough. Gio bears the brunt of the stress. I guess that's probably the reason he comes across as the world's biggest asshole most times.

I wouldn't be lining up to take over the De Bellis empire anytime soon. That's for damn sure. Our father and his father before him built this world we live in. It's full of nothing but blood, filth, death. Oh, and bucketloads of fucking money. Which is why we all do it, right?

I'm convinced somewhere along the way, the old man made a deal with a witch and now our bloodline is cursed for eternity. I don't see any of us getting a happily ever after. Our world isn't a place for women. Well, not the nice kind. Not the type of girls you'd want to spend the rest of your life with.

Santo, the second in line to the throne so to speak, is the reason we're here tonight. Tomorrow is his wedding day. He's marrying his childhood sweetheart. It's supposed to be his one night to let loose. He's meant to be enjoying his last day of freedom.

I can tell he's counting down the hours until he gets to see Shelli, though. Guy doesn't give a shit about the ass handed to him on a silver fucking platter in this club. I gave up warning him about the curse years ago. My gut is telling me this whole wedding thing is going to blow up in our faces, but I'm not about to try to stop it.

I mean, who knows? Santo and Shelli might just be the ones to break the curse.

"You haven't so much as glanced at all the tits and ass on the stage right now. If this expensive wedding bullshit has made you too broke to afford a lap dance, bro, I got you. My shout. Fuck, take one to the back room for a happy ending," I direct to Santo, pulling out my wallet and throwing four large bills onto the table.

"Put your cash away. Unlike you fuckers, I don't need to pay for pussy. And why would I want *this*, when I have Shelli waiting for me back at the hotel?" Santo counters.

"Ah, because it's your last night as a free man. And what the fuck do you mean she's waiting for you at the hotel? It's bad luck to see the bride the night before the wedding, bro," Vin reminds him.

Vin is the baby of the family. Kid's seventeen, in his final year of high school. And the only reason he's sitting in our club right now—so clearly underage—is because of his last name. That and the fact we own the joint.

"She sent me a text and said she had something important to talk about. Told her I'd stop by her room when we got back." Santo shrugs.

A waitress wearing nothing but a thin black thong and sky-high heels approaches the table with a new bottle of whiskey before refilling each of our glasses. "Sweetheart, my brother here is getting hitched tomorrow. Help me convince him he should have one last hurrah," I tell her.

"Married, huh? Well, if I knew that, I would have brought out the good stuff. But he's right. You definitely need to have a little fun before you tie the knot." The girl then manoeuvres around to my brother. Leaning forward and pressing her bare tits into his face as she whispers something into his ear.

Santo doesn't bite, though. He simply shakes his head and gently pushes her back a step. I wonder if Shelli knows just how fucking lucky she is. My brother is as loyal as they come.

"You know, I'm getting married too," Gabe chimes in, and we all look at him. "What? I am. One day, when I find a girl worthy of keeping my balls in her purse." He smirks and pushes to his feet. "Come on, babe. You can show me all the filthy things you just offered to do to him. The difference is... *I'll* actually enjoy them." He takes the girl's hand and disappears with her through the crowd.

At least one of us is going to enjoy the night. I pick up my tumbler of whiskey and down it in one go. "I'm out. Catch all you fuckers in the morning," I tell my brothers as I push up from my seat.

"Where the fuck are you going?" Gio grunts at me.

"Somewhere else." I shrug. I don't tell him that this place is about as exciting as watching paint dry. I don't need the questions that would follow. I'm sure each and every one of my brothers would love to know what's going on in my head.

Strippers have never done it for me. Personally, I don't see the appeal. I used to wonder if I was broken. I've watched guy after guy get aroused the moment they step foot in one of our clubs.

Me? I've never had so much as a twitch while watching these women dance. I've faked interest enough times, flirted and put on a good show, but I've never fucked any of 'em. It's not that I don't love women. I do. *I really fucking do.* I just have standards. I'm picky when it comes to where I stick my dick.

I push out of the club doors. Turn and walk down the street. There's a small bar a few blocks up that serves Cinque. If I'm going to be drinking tonight, I only want the best. And the shit my brothers and I blend is the best damn whiskey you'll ever taste.

It's the one and only business that's ours through and through. Our father has nothing to do with it. I guess that's what drove all of us to make it the success it is. The old man laughed in our faces when we brought up the idea of investing in a distillery. And then, when he discovered what we were on to, he tried to push his way in. Take the reins.

Thankfully, that didn't happen. Don't get me wrong, the old fuck is one hell of a businessman. No one gets where he is without knowing what they're doing. The problem with him, though, is that he turns everything dirty.

De Bellis Cinque is clean, and my brothers and I plan to keep it that way. Not that any of us are on the path to a straight and narrow life. This business is just our one outlier. A passion project that doesn't need to be tainted by our father and his associates.

The first drops of rain hit me as I push through

the door of the bar. Fucking Melbourne weather. One minute you're sweating your ass off, and the next you need a fucking coat to stave off the chill. It's unpredictable. But I wouldn't move from this city for anything in the world. I fucking love it here.

Being one of the five princes of the underground doesn't hurt either. There isn't anything or anyone I can't have in this city. If I want it, I'm going to get it and usually with ease. It's one of the perks of bearing my last name.

I drop into one of the stools at the end of the counter and the barman gives me a nod of acknowledgement before he picks up a Cinque bottle, bringing it and a glass over and placing them in front of me.

"Marcel, thought you'd be busy with your brothers tonight," Brian says.

"They're boring, so I came here. Thought I'd let you entertain me for a bit, B." I smirk at him.

I've been coming here since before I was legally old enough to drink. Brian is an old associate of my father's. How that man has any friends I'll never know. The fact everyone is scared of the asshole is more than likely what keeps people in his corner. Better the devil you know and all that.

"It's busy," I comment while my eyes bounce around the usually quiet bar.

"Yeah, some asshole posted one of those video things you kids are all obsessed with and now these young idiots keep flooding in," Brian grunts with a shake of his head.

I laugh. "You went viral, mate. Most people would kill to have that sort of attention on their business."

"Yeah, I'm not most people." Brian walks off to serve another customer.

Picking up the bottle of Cinque, I pour myself a healthy serving in the crystal tumbler. Whiskey like ours should be savoured. Sipped. Usually. Tonight, I down the entire contents before refilling my glass again.

I need a buzz, something to distract me from the sense of imminent doom I've got going on in my gut. Something real shitty is about to happen. I don't know what it is. I guess I'll find out when it happens.

I'm on my fourth glass when my gaze sweeps to the door just as it opens and a woman walks in looking like a deer caught in the headlights. I chuckle before I can stop myself. The guys in here are going to eat her alive. Although, judging by the look on her face which tells me she's contemplating walking straight back out the door, I think she knows that.

Long blonde hair hangs down to her waist, damp from the downpour that's going on outside. Thick, pouty lips painted red—bet they'd feel fucking amazing wrapped around my dick.

Speaking of, he's finally woken up and paying attention, thanks to the woman who just walked in. I told you I had a type, and she's it. She's tiny. There's not much of her, and I imagine if I were standing next to her, I'd tower over her small frame.

I watch her like a hunter eyeing his prey as she tentatively approaches the bar. She's nervous, her hands twisting around the straps of her purse. Chanel, huh? Little trust-fund brat, no doubt. Brian notices her the moment she takes a seat and walks over. I can't hear what they're saying to each other. Which pisses me off. I need to get closer.

As soon as a cocktail glass filled with red liquid is placed in front of her, some asshole is already on her. I can see her discomfort as he crowds her space, trapping her between his body and the bar. I slide off my stool and walk over, my hands fisting at my sides.

"Hey, babe. Sorry I'm late." I wink at her before turning my attention to the fucker pushing himself against her chair. "Mind backing the fuck away from my girl?" I growl at him.

The guy's eyes widen as he steps aside with his hands up, then practically runs in the opposite direction.

I sit on the stool next to the woman as my lips curl into a smirk. "Like I was saying, sorry I'm late. I got held up at the office."

Chapter Two

One hour earlier

"A rgh!" I throw my curling iron down onto the vanity. Why am I bothering? What on earth was I thinking? I can't just go out and hook up with some rando for one night. Can I?

I want to. I want to be that girl. The kind who can let go and have a little fun. I want to be the girl who doesn't come with enough baggage to fill an Amazon warehouse. And we all know how big those places are. I wish I could be carefree. Live in the moment. Have flings. Enjoy an orgasm that wasn't brought on by myself.

I've accepted the fact that I'm not girlfriend material. My one and only failed relationship is proof of that. I tried. I really did. I actually liked Flynn. I met him a few months after I moved to Melbourne, with every intention of starting fresh. A new me, new life sort of thing.

It didn't work. I was too much for him. I couldn't hide myself from him, no matter how hard I tried. Eventually, he saw the ugly parts of me, the things that haunt me not only at night but also in broad daylight.

I remember the first time I panicked in front of him. He freaked out, and I didn't hear from him for two weeks after the incident. I tried to assure him that I was fine, that I was healing from a traumatic event. I didn't elaborate on what that event was for obvious reasons.

Turns out, I liked Flynn more than he liked me. Because he only stuck around for six months before he broke things off. Telling me I was too damaged and that I'm never going to be normal.

It stung. But I got the message loud and freaking clear. That was a year ago. I haven't thought about dating or anything close since. Now, I'm ready to put myself back out there. Well, I'm ready to *try* to put myself out there.

I figure I can just have sex. People do it all the time. I don't need a relationship for that. And I enjoyed having sex with Flynn. I didn't know if I would, but he was gentle and sweet in the bedroom. Which was exactly what I needed.

Now, I just need to try. Right?

I pick up my phone and call Izzy. My... I guess you could call her my unofficially adoptive mother. She and her husband took me into their home, into their family, when I was seventeen. They didn't adopt me legally. But Mikhail did help me change my last name, insisted that I become a Petrov.

I owe everything to Izzy and Mikhail. If they hadn't found me when they did, I probably wouldn't be alive today. I don't know if I would have been strong enough to withstand the torment my life had become. The life I was sold into.

Yes, sold. Like I said, I'm recovering from a traumatic event, or rather a series of events. I'm never going to fully recover. I know that, but I refuse to curl up into a ball and cry in the corner. The Petrovs have given me a second chance at life, a chance not many girls like me get. A chance I'm not going to waste.

Which is why two years ago, when Savannah Valentino (one of Izzy's familial connections) set me up with a job in Melbourne, I jumped at the chance to leave New York and start over. And I haven't looked back. Being in a different city was exactly the change I needed.

Not that I didn't love living with the Petrovs. I did. But I couldn't live with them forever. I had to grow up eventually. Although Mikhail would totally jump at the chance for me to return home. The man is every bit the protective father I never had.

The ringtone stops on my phone's speaker before it's replaced by Izzy's voice. "Well, hello, stranger."

"Hey, I didn't wake you, did I?" I ask her.

"No, baby did. Hours ago. But even if you had, I wouldn't care. What are you doing? Ready to come home?"

"Always ready to come home. But I can't right now. Work is busy."

"It always is." Izzy sighs.

I understand her frustration. I haven't stepped

foot in New York since I left. Izzy and Mikhail have come to visit me in Melbourne. A lot. I feel bad that they have to make such a long flight with little ones. They have three now, Mabilia, Neo... and little Lex, who I've yet to meet.

"How's the baby?" I ask.

"Perfect," Izzy says. "You should come home and let him meet his big sister."

"I will, soon."

"Okay. What else is happening in the world of the diaper-free life you're living?"

"So I was thinking... Wait... Is Mikhail listening?" No way am I telling my adoptive father what I'm planning to do tonight. He'd have his little Russian soldiers stop over and lock me away in some tower.

"No, why? What are you doing, Zoe?" Izzy sounds more intrigued now.

"I'm going out," I say. "I was thinking I could, you know, go out. Meet someone, just for the night."

"Oh my god! You're going out to hook up? A one-night stand?" she squeals.

"Well, I thought I was, but now I'm not so sure I can go through with it." I sigh.

"You can do anything you want to do. Is this something you *want*?"

"I want to. Or I want to try. See if I can, you know." I pick up the red tube and line my lips.

"I get it. I think you should go out and see what happens. Don't have any preconceived notions in your head of what's going to happen. Just go to a bar, order a drink, and see where the night takes you," Izzy says.

"You're right. I can do that." I smile while straightening my shoulders. *I can do this.*

"You can. But make sure you have protection. Condoms, pistol, knife." Izzy lists off everything that's already in my bag.

"I know. I've got it all."

"Good. You know the last one-night stand I had was with Mikhail," she tells me.

I've heard that story so many times already. She and Mikhail hooked up some night in a bar. They were from rival families—though they didn't know it at the time. And then, well, the rest is history.

"Thanks, Iz. You always know what to say." She really does. I feel way better about my decision now.

"Anytime, Zoe. Just be smart and safe," she reminds me. "But also have fun."

"I will. Love you."

"Ti amo," she replies.

I think the universe is sending me a sign, seeing as the sky decided to open up on me the moment I stepped out of the car. I rush through the door of the closest bar. I was planning to walk up and down this strip and then decide on a place to try out this whole *seeing where the night goes* thing.

But as soon as I step inside the bar, I start second-guessing my decision. I can't do this. The place is crowded. I can feel my skin crawling. Itching. It's the first sign that I'm about to panic.

I take a deep breath and dig my nails into my palms. I will not panic. I can do this. Then I force my legs to take step by step until I reach the counter. I just need a drink. Maybe after a bit of alcohol, I'll have the courage to actually sit here longer than five minutes.

"Hey, sweetheart, what'll it be?" a barman asks, his forearms resting against the wooden top as he leans over to meet my eyes.

"Um, just a cosmopolitan, please," I ask him.

"Sure thing," he says before spinning around. I

spend the next few minutes taking in the bar's interior.

I can do this, I repeat to myself.

I'm already sitting on a stool. At a bar. I've just ordered a drink. And I don't feel like I need to run for the hills.

The bartender places a glass in front of me. "Here you go, sweetheart," he says with an encouraging smile.

"Thank you." I pick up the glass, bring it to my lips, and sip at the sweet concoction. I'm not a huge drinker, but I do know a couple of these and I'll be way more relaxed.

Something presses against my side. Not something, *someone*. I lower my glass, slowly placing it back on the counter. Pivoting in my seat with my hand on my bag. I can reach for something, anything, if the need arises. Although I think turning around was a big mistake when a man pushes closer to me. Practically trapping me between him and the edge of the bar.

I do my best not to panic. I'm safe. This bar is full of people. Nothing is going to happen to me with all these people here to witness it.

"I haven't seen you here before. What's your name?" the guy asks.

My eyes dart around the room, searching for an escape. I need to get this man away from me. He reeks of beer. It's disgusting. How anyone can think it's attractive, I have no idea.

Before I can respond, ask him to take a step back, another man shows up, pushing his way between the first guy and me.

"Hey, babe. Sorry I'm late," he says with a wink, while my glare is hooked on a pair of dark-brown eyes until he isn't looking at me anymore. Instead, his attention is on the other man. "Mind backing the fuck away from my girl?"

The next thing I know, the first guy disappears into the crowd. And then, as if nothing happened, my new self-proclaimed boyfriend, who smells nothing like beer and everything like whiskey and citrus, sits on the stool next to mine and smiles. "Like I was saying, sorry I'm late. I got held up at the office."

I glance to my left. Surely he's not talking to me, but when I return my attention his way, he just keeps smiling. "Do I know you?" I ask in a low tone.

"I'm Marcel." He holds out a palm.

I look at his hand. His large, tanned hand. Before tentatively placing my much smaller palm in his. "Zoe."

"So, Zoe, did you know that wanker or am I like your knight in shining armour, saving you from spending the rest of your evening trying to evade him?" Marcel smirks.

"First, you didn't save me. I could have saved myself." I sit up straighter. One of the many things I learned from Izzy was to never let a man think you need him. Another? Don't rely on being saved. Help yourself. Fight for yourself with everything you have.

"I have no doubt." Marcel picks up a crystal glass from the counter. Where did that even come from? Before it reaches his lips, he tilts his head. "Just out of curiosity, how were you planning on saving yourself?"

I smile. "Well, let's see. I could have shot him in the balls with the pistol I'm hiding in my bag." I pause, waiting for his reaction. The guy doesn't flinch. Doesn't even glance at the bag I'm still clutching in my hand. "Or if I was worried about the noise, there's always the small blade I have within arm's reach. I could have gone right for his neck. That would be messy, though."

"And a bullet to the balls wouldn't be?" Marcel laughs.

"I guess you're right, but it would be much more

satisfying." I swipe up my drink from the bar top and gulp down a mouthful.

"I don't know... Watching the fucker bleed out on the floor, flailing around and holding his neck would be pretty satisfying too."

"Maybe." I shrug.

"Is that what you do, Zoe? Go around to bars, looking for some helpless guy you can lure back to your lair to cut open?"

"It isn't, but now that you mentioned it, it could be a good career move." I smirk. "Rewarding even. Want to be my first client?"

"As long as the knife doesn't hit anywhere lethal." He lifts a single shoulder. "I'm always down for an adventure."

I laugh, and for the first time since this whole idea got into my head, I feel myself relax. It's easy talking to Marcel. There's something about him. Something that just, I don't know, puts me at ease. Makes me feel like I'm safe with him. Which I know is a stupid thought. I don't know the guy.

But I don't need to know him to have fun with him, do I?

Chapter Three

I've been talking to Zoe for an hour. I don't recall the last time I ever just *talked* to someone for a whole hour. Fuck, I need to either seal the deal with this chick or break ties. At least that's what I'd usually be doing.

I'm honestly happy just sitting here talking to her. It's... refreshing to talk to a woman who either doesn't know who I am or doesn't give a shit. She's not trying to get anything out of me. She argued when I told Brian to put her drinks on my tab.

"So, are you going to invite me back to your place at some point tonight?" Zoe asks.

Whiskey gets caught in my throat and I choke down a lungful. "Shit," I hiss, trying to catch my breath. That was literally the last thing I expected to come out of her mouth.

"Oh my god, I'm so sorry. I just assumed... Well, I shouldn't have. Forget I said anything."

"Don't be sorry," I tell her. "Let's go." I jump up and hold out a hand. I won't drag her out of here like the neanderthal I want to be. She needs to make the conscious—okay, tipsy—decision to come with me.

Zoe takes my hand and slides off her stool. She's even tinier than I thought. Her head doesn't even reach my shoulder. "Where are we going?" she asks.

"I have a hotel room at the Four Seasons. My brother's getting married tomorrow. We're all supposed to stay there tonight."

"Your brother? Why aren't you with him?"

"Because my brothers, all four of them, are a hell of a lot less exciting than you are, Zoe. Which means I'd much rather hang out with you."

Her hand grips mine a little tighter as we work our way through the crowds on the sidewalk.

I glance in her direction. Her lips are pressed tight together. "You okay?"

"I'm fine. I just don't like crowds all that much," she says.

"Me either," I admit.

I guide Zoe through the lobby of the Four Seasons and straight to the lifts, my cock hardening more and more with every minute it takes to get back to my room. I want to get inside this woman. Now. As soon as the doors open onto my floor, I reach out and toss her over my shoulder before making my way down the corridor.

"What the hell?" Zoe screams while slapping her open palms across my back. "I will shoot you, you know."

"I figured this was the fastest way to get things done." I tap the key card on the door, push it open, and let it slam behind me before tossing her onto the bed this time. "I want you naked."

I slide my arms out of my jacket, dropping it to the floor as I make quick work of unfastening the buttons on my shirt. My cufflinks land on the plush carpet, followed by my shirt. "You're not naked yet, Zoe," I tell her.

She hasn't moved from her spot on the bed. Slowly, so fucking slowly, she climbs off the mattress and shimmies herself out of her dress. While I kick off my shoes, bend forward, and remove my socks. My eyes stay glued to Zoe, who is standing in front of me in a matching light-pink lace bra and panty set. And a pair of sky-high black heels.

Fuck, I love those shoes.

"Leave the heels," I tell her when she goes to kick them off. Then I step closer to her, my hands grabbing for my belt and tugging it loose. "Leave all of it. I've changed my mind. You're like a fucking present and I want the pleasure of unwrapping you myself." My fingers slide to the button of my slacks before I pull down the fly. Then I reach out a hand and brush it along her collarbone. "Do you have any idea how fucking good you look right now?"

"No." Her eyes drop to the carpet.

Placing my fingers under her jaw, I lift her chin, forcing her gaze to meet mine. "You've never seen a mirror? Fuck, babe, you should know I'll be jerking off to this image of you for years to come." I move my mouth closer to hers. "Trust me when I say my cock doesn't get hard for just anyone. But you, Zoe, you've got me harder than I've been in a long time." I close the gap and slam my lips onto hers.

I've been dying to kiss her all fucking night. My hands move around to her back, one cupping her head, the other resting on that dip right above her ass. Zoe's lips part and I take the invitation, walking us backwards until we're falling onto the bed. Where my body hovers above hers.

"Do you want me to touch you, Zoe? Do you want me to make you come harder than you've ever come before?"

Zoe's cheeks flush a bright pink as she nods her head.

"That's not going to work for me, babe. I need you to use your words. Tell me you want me to touch you. That you want me to fuck you."

"I want you to fuck me, Marcel. I feel like I'm going to combust if you don't touch me. Please," she says.

"With fucking pleasure," I growl before taking her mouth again.

Our tongues duel for ownership. This is one fight she won't win, though. I'm going to own this tight little body of hers by the end of the night. There won't be an inch of her I haven't explored with my fingers, my tongue, my cock. My hand slides under her back, unhooking her bra before I push myself upright. Then I drag the straps over her shoulders and her perky breasts bounce free. They're not huge but they're not small either. They're just fucking right. And real. So fucking real.

Filling each of my palms with one of her breasts, I massage the soft globes before leaning down and taking one of her rosy nipples into my mouth. Sucking it between my teeth, I bite down slightly, my eyes focused on her face. Watching. Waiting for her every reaction.

Her eyes widen. But it's the way her legs try to close, squeezing each side of my thighs, that tells me just how much she loved that little tinge of pain. I lick at her nipple. "Fuck, you have great tits," I tell her.

Zoe's hands tangle in the ends of my hair. "Mhmm," she moans as I continue to show her breasts the attention they deserve. Moving down her body, I stop when my mouth hovers over her panty-covered pussy. She's wet. I smell her arousal. See the wetness seeping through the fabric.

"Are you wet for me, Zoe?" I ask her.

She nods her head.

"I can't hear you. I might just have to find out for myself." My fingers slide under the fabric of her underwear, gliding through her wet folds. "Fucking soaked. This all for me, babe?"

Zoe looks at me. Directly into my eyes. "Yes," she says, her head falling back onto the mattress when I press a finger on her clit.

I slide my hands over, fist the side of her panties, and rip them. Shoving the material out of the way so that I now have full access to her pussy. "Fuck me. You're gorgeous," I growl before lowering my head. I place a featherlight kiss at the top of her pussy lips.

Her hands grip my head as soon as my tongue makes contact with her slit. Sliding up from the bottom to the top. I push two fingers into her while my tongue continues to lap at her clit.

"Oh god, that's so good," Zoe moans. I want to ride this out for as long as I can, but I also just really want to see her fucking come.

I go in hard, licking and sucking like my life depends on it. Her body is squirming beneath me, her head shaking back and forth. Everything about this woman is intoxicating. I feel like I'm drunk on the smell and taste of her.

"Fuck, you're tight. This pretty pussy of yours is going to choke my cock so fucking good." I feel her walls tighten around my fingers, her body responding to every filthy word that leaves my mouth.

Pumping my fingers in and out, I curve them

inside, finding that one spot that never fails to send a woman wild. My mouth closes over her clit, my tongue swirling around the hardened bud as I lick and suck with an enthusiasm I've never had while going down on someone before. Her entire body tenses, her pussy squeezing the fuck out of my fingers, so hard I honestly think she could break them.

Then her screams echo off the walls of the room "Oh god! Shit! Oh my god!"

I don't stop. My fingers continue to pump in and out, my tongue licking at her clit until she comes down and her body completely relaxes. "That was the sexiest fucking thing I've seen." I grin as I push up off the mattress.

I shove my pants down my legs, quickly followed by my boxers, freeing my cock. My fists wrap around it, pulling a few times while I bend and reach into my back pocket for my wallet. Retrieving a condom, I open the foil with my teeth and roll the protection down my shaft. Before settling back between Zoe's legs again.

I look into her eyes. There's lust there but there's also something else. Fear. I know that look all too fucking well, and it's not one I want to see on the chick I'm about to fuck.

"You okay?"

Zoe nods her head, but her mouth stays firmly shut.

"We don't have to do this, you know. *You* don't have to do this," I say while shifting my weight to one arm and sliding off her.

Zoe's arms reach out and close around my neck. "I want to. I do. It's just... been a while, and you... Well, *it's* not exactly small."

"My ego or my cock?" I grin.

"Both." She laughs.

"I'll go slow. If at any time you need to stop, just tell me, okay? And I will stop. Promise." I would never force myself on a woman. Ever. I'm all sorts of fucked up, but I'm not that. Lining my cock up with her entrance, I push inside her. Gently. Taking my time. Making sure she's enjoying this as much as I am. "Fuck, is this what heaven feels like?" I lean my face down, claim her lips, and ever so fucking slowly glide my cock all the way in. Once I'm buried to the hilt, I feel her tense. I stop moving and grit my teeth. "You okay?"

"Uh-huh, you feel... good." She sighs.

"Oh, babe, I'm about to make you feel so fucking good you'll forget your own name." I smirk as I drag my cock out before slamming back in again. Gradually picking up my pace. Reaching between our bodies, I circle her clit with my thumb. "I need you to come again. I want to feel you come on my cock," I tell her.

I pump faster. Harder. Her body matching my rhythm as her hips lift off the bed to meet mine. "Don't stop. Oh god, don't fucking stop," she screams out.

Leaning forward, I bite her earlobe. "The night is only just beginning," I whisper. I'm going to make her come at least twice more before I'm done with her.

Zoe's entire body stiffens. The walls of her pussy tighten around me. She tips her head back and screams my name as she comes apart.

Fuck, that's tight.

I didn't want to come yet. But I can feel the tingling sensation crawling up my spine. My balls tighten, my movements ruthless as I drive into her while chasing my own fucking orgasm before following her into the abyss.

"That was... Oh god, what the hell was that?" Zoe asks, throwing an arm over her eyes.

I roll off her, lying next to her on the bed as both of our chests rise and fall in quick succession. "*That* was perfect fucking, Zoe. You and me, we're going to have one hell of a night, babe."

Chapter Four

"**G**et up. You gotta go," a deep, gravelly voice breaks through my sleep-fogged brain.

"Huh?" I slowly blink my eyes open.

"Your time here has expired. I got shit to do, and you're not it. Sorry, sweetheart, but you have to leave."

I glance at the guy sprawled out next to me in bed and want to rip that smirk off his too-pretty face.

"You're a fucking asshole," I hiss at him. "And you fuck like a preteen getting pussy for the first time." I jump out of bed, suddenly wide awake, as I snatch last night's dress and bra from the floor.

I can feel his eyes on me. I'm completely naked, but I remember everything. I wasn't that drunk. And even though he's an asshole, he's a safe asshole. He's not going to hurt me. Not physically anyway. Just with his sharp words it seems. I don't know how I know that. But I do.

"That's not what you were saying last night when you were screaming my name," Marcel says.

I turn a seething glare on him. "Don't flatter yourself. I was just giving you what you wanted to hear. I'm a people pleaser." I smile, pivot on my heel, and walk into the adjoining bathroom. Slamming the door shut before locking it. If he wants me to leave, I will. But not until after I shower.

I take my time too. The water pressure is next level. Besides, knowing that Marcel wants me to get out of his room, well, that only makes me more defiant.

Then a thought hits me. I did it. I went out. I went home with someone, well, to a hotel anyway.

And I had a one-night stand. I actually did it. And the sex. I'll take it to my grave, certainly never admit it out loud, but the sex was mind-blowing.

After I've had my fill of his hot water, I towel dry my hair and throw my clothes back on, sans underwear. Thanks to the asshole who destroyed them. Although, at the time, I have to admit it was kind of hot. I find a comb in his toiletries bag and use it to rake through my damp hair. I refuse to walk out of this hotel looking like shit.

"The water pressure's good, by the way," I hum as I walk out of the bathroom, reach down, and pick up my discarded bag from the floor. Then I slide my feet into my heels, turn, and walk out of the bedroom.

"Wait," Marcel yells out after me.

"What?" My palm is already wrapped around the handle. Ready to yank the door open and get the hell out of here.

"I, uh, I didn't catch your name," he says, raking a hand through his hair.

Yes, he did. He just doesn't remember it. Which is probably for the best.

"No, you didn't," I lie, instead of correcting him. Guess he was drunker than I thought. Though he didn't seem to be. "See you around, Marcello. Or not." I've spent enough time around Izzy's side of the family to know his full name and how to use it. Then I tug open the door. Only to have my worlds colliding.

"Zoe, what the fuck?"

Shit. God, no. This cannot be happening to me. Now, of all times.

"Dom? What the fuck are you doing here?" Marcel asks from behind me.

Dominic McKinley, Lucy's fiancée. The same Lucy who happens to be my boss and friend. Oh, and there's also the fact that Dom is like a cousin to me. It's complicated, but his family tree is tied to the Valentinos. Specifically, he's related to Izzy's cousins. Which means me being here. In this hotel room. With Marcel. Could very well get back to Mikhail.

My one-night stand might be an asshole but I don't want the guy dead. Hurt, maybe. But dead? No.

"Marcello, really? Fuck, it was nice knowing you, bro." Dom laughs while shaking his head.

"You didn't see me here. You don't know me. I'm out." I point to Dom, quickly pushing past him before making my way out of the room and down the hall. I'm not sticking around to be interrogated. And

I really don't wanna know how those two know each other.

As if on cue, just as I disconnect my call with Izzy, the doorbell rings out. My adoptive mom literally stayed up just to hear how my night went. I told her that I met Marcel, not in as much detail as she wanted, and purposely left out his name.

Dropping my phone onto the coffee table, I get up and walk to the front door, which is already swinging open before I can reach it. Lucy steps inside with a look that says "I know what you did last night" written all over her face.

I'm honestly surprised it took her this long to turn up. I thought for sure I would have heard from her within thirty minutes of leaving the hotel this morning.

I hold up my hands, stopping her when she opens her mouth. "Before you start, I just want to say one thing."

"Fine. What?" she asks while turning to close my front door.

"I…" Shit, what do I say? "I don't want to talk about it." I pivot on my heel and stalk back into the living room, throwing myself far too dramatically onto the sofa.

"Too bad. This is way too juicy not to talk about." Lucy sits next to me, a hundred times more ladylike than I just did. Placing her bag on the coffee table, she shifts her body towards me. "You had sex!" she squeals in an ungodly high-pitched tone. "And with a De Bellis at that," she adds.

"A what now?" I narrow my eyes at her.

"A De Bellis brother, the hot one too. Well, technically, they're all hot. But don't tell Dom I said that," she's quick to clarify. "Marcel, though? That man is fine with a capital F-I-N-E. Zoe, you had sex with Marcello De Bellis."

"Shh, the whole neighbourhood does not need to hear my business." I jump across and cover her mouth with my hand. Lucy sticks her tongue out, licking my palm. "Ew, gross." I pull my arm back and wipe my hand against her pants.

"Like I was saying, you had sex with Marcel. So?" she asks, not missing a beat.

"So what?"

"Don't play coy with me, Zoe Petrov. Was it good? Was *he* good?"

"Good sex is really perception based. Like what I might think is good, you might think is mediocre, right? So how do I know if it was good or I just haven't experienced really great sex yet?"

That's it, Zoe, I cheer myself on. *Deflect, deflect, deflect.*

"Dom is the best sex I've ever had. Ever will have. That man is... Well, it's beyond good." Lucy looks off into the distance before shaking her head and refocusing on me. I am not going to ask where her thoughts just went. "Anyway, did he make you come?"

"Yes."

"More than once?"

"Yes."

"And you're sitting here questioning if it was good?"

"No, I'm just saying what I thought was good could be different from what you think is good," I repeat. "Do you want a drink? Coffee? Tea?" As I go to stand, Lucy grabs my arm.

"Not so fast. Fine. Let's try it your way. In your opinion, was it good? Wait... Was he... Did he treat you right? Because if he didn't, I'm going to feed him to Dom's pigs myself." She grinds her teeth.

"He was plenty nice last night. But I guess sometime between last night and this morning, my prince turned back into a frog. Or rather, an ass."

"What'd he do?"

"Woke me up and told me that *my time had expired* or some shit like that." My jaw clenches at the memory. It's not like I wanted to stay. I don't care if I ever see him again, but he didn't have to be such an asshole about it.

"He what?" Lucy jumps up from the sofa, her arms thrown in the air. "I'm going to skin him alive. I don't even care if he's Dom's only friend."

"Wait... How friendly are we talking here? How come I've never heard of him before?"

"I've never had a reason to bring him up." She shrugs. "And, honestly, a De Bellis brother would be one of the last people on earth I'd think you'd climb into bed with."

"You keep saying that. De Bellis. What is that?"

"Marcello's last name. His family is... Well, they're kind of a big deal in Melbourne's underground."

"He's in the mob?" I groan.

"His family, yeah," Lucy confirms.

Of all the people in this city...

"Oh god! Izzy and Mikhail cannot find out about

this," I tell Lucy. "Make sure Dom doesn't tell anyone else. Please."

"I've already threatened him. He won't say anything. Dom's not much of a talker anyway," she says.

"What'd you threaten him with?" I ask her.

"You really don't want to know," Lucy says. "How about that drink? You could probably use one yourself. You know, after all that hot sex last night." She winks at me.

"I didn't say it was hot sex," I groan.

"You didn't say it wasn't either. And it's Marcel. Which means it was definitely hot sex." She laughs.

"It really was," I admit while covering my face. "But it was a onetime thing. It's not happening again. I went out to see if I could do it. If I could actually have a one-night stand. And I did." I smile. I'm honestly really damn happy that I didn't crumble. I did it.

"Hell yes! You do you, girl." Lucy follows me into the kitchen.

I set the kettle on, then turn around again. Lucy's eyes are glued to her phone. Her face is pale. "What's wrong?" I ask her.

"Dom just messaged me," she says, not looking up from the screen.

"Lucy, you're scaring me. What happened?" I cross the kitchen, closing the distance between us.

"It's Shelli... She was murdered."

I frown, trying to recall if I've ever met anyone named Shelli. I don't think I have.

"She was Santo's fiancée. They were getting married today. I was meant to be meeting Dom at the church in a few hours." Lucy peers up at me. "Marcello's future sister-in-law was murdered last night."

I have this sudden urge to find Marcel and find out if he's okay, but that's stupid. He literally kicked me out of his hotel room this morning, and then there's the fact that I don't even know the guy. Why would he want some random chick he hooked up bothering him at a time when his family is in mourning?

"That's awful. Is there anything I can do? Did you know her?"

"I met her a few times. I didn't know her all that well. But she always seemed nice. What I do know is how much in love they were. This is going to destroy Santo."

"I don't even know what to say. I couldn't imagine that happening on the day you're supposed to get married."

"I know. Me either." Lucy types something into her phone.

"How... I mean... Do you think..." *Crap, what am I even asking?*

"Dom's with Marcel now. He's not in a good way," Lucy says, as if reading my mind.

For some reason, I don't like that he's hurting. I shouldn't care. He didn't seem to care when he was throwing me out of his room this morning. Why the hell should I care if he's hurting?

But I do, and I hate that I do.

Chapter Five

Two weeks later

I have no idea why I'm here. Except for the fact that I need an escape from reality right now. Because the reality is... I just buried my father. A father my brother killed. A father I'm not mourning one fucking bit.

Santo, though. He's fucking hurting, and that's what's hurting me. Shelli was everything to him. Then to lose her... to find out our father killed her. I can't imagine what's going on in his head. And I can't do a single fucking thing to fix it.

Gio killed the old man, then burned our fucking house down. Now, we're all staying in his penthouse in the city. It's cramped. Five men in one penthouse. The place is huge, but it's not the kind of space we're used to having. At the same time, everyone is mourning the loss of Shelli. She was like a sister to us.

We're also trying to figure out the best way to help Santo. Gio doesn't want our brother left alone. Afraid Santo'll try to do something he can't undo. Basically, he's on suicide watch. The rest of us taking turns monitoring him. I can't say I don't blame Gio for that decision. I've never seen Santo so... destroyed.

I guess the old man finally did it. He's been trying to destroy us since the day we were born. And now, it's as if the light that used to burn bright within Santo is switched off, and I'm not sure it'll ever return. My brother was the glass half-full kind of guy. Always positive, always looking for good in people. He's lost... I just hope one of us can find a way to help him navigate a life without Shelli in it.

Which is why I'm here. Sitting outside of Zoe's house, wondering if I should go in or not. I don't know why I'm so drawn to this woman. Ever since the morning I kicked her out of my bed, I wanted to drag her back into it. It's fucked up. I can't get the chick out of my damn head. Doesn't matter what I'm doing lately. Attending funerals, dealing with the shitshow that is life at the moment. All I want is to drown myself in her.

I know the right thing to do is walk away. If I stay around her too fucking long, the curse is going to touch her too. I've already seen what it's done to Santo and Shelli.

None of that seems to change the fact that I'm here. Just one more time. I don't need to see her again after this. I can fuck her out of my head and get on with my life. With this in mind, I step out of my car and walk across the street.

I've been watching her house for hours. I know she's in there. I've seen her through some of the windows. The moment I realised Dom knew her, I started digging. It didn't take long. Dom has connections in the States. More specifically, a connection with the Valentinos. And Zoe's accent screamed New Yorker. After that, I just had to find a Zoe with ties to the Valentinos. And there was only one of those.

Zoe Petrov.

What intrigued me the most was where that trail ended. Prior to a few years ago, *Zoe Petrov* didn't exist. All I know is that she lived with Mikhail Petrov, the Russian Pakhan. A scary motherfucker. I mean, the guy married into one of the five Italian families of New York, *as a Russian,* and survived. The real puzzle is how does Zoe fit into those two families? The Valentinos and the Petrovs.

She's neither Italian nor Russian. That much is clear. But here she is, living in a house most twenty-somethings would never be able to afford. At first, I thought she was joking when she mentioned shooting that guy in the bar. Now, I'm not so sure.

Not that it makes much of a difference to me. I don't need to know how she fits into those crime families. It doesn't matter. Because I'm not going to know her all that long. I can't get attached to a woman. It'll only end in disaster for them.

My endeavours are singular in nature. It's what I do. It makes everything easier.

I approach Zoe's front door, reaching out a hand to ring the bell, and wait. I briefly considered letting myself in. It wouldn't be all that hard. I've already seen the layout of this house. I was tempted to hack into the security cameras but figured that'd be crossing the line. Although I know that's what Dom did when he was stalking... I mean courting Lucy. Worked out pretty well for him.

The door swings open and I have to school the surprise on my face. Fuck, she's hotter than I remembered. Zoe's wearing one of those sundresses with the thin straps, white with yellow sunflowers printed on it. What she's not wearing is a bra. I can see her nipples. They're basically begging my mouth to wrap around them.

It's not her dress that surprises me, though. It's the pistol she's holding in her outstretched hand. The pistol she's pointing directly at me. My dick hardens. Why the fuck am I turned on by the image of her threatening me? That's something no amount of shrinks will ever be able to unpack.

I raise my eyebrows. "Do you always answer the door with such hospitality?"

"What are you doing here, Marcel? And how did you find my house?" she asks, not moving that gun an inch.

"I'm here because I wanted to see you. That's usually why people visit other people, babe. You gonna invite me in, or are we going to stand here pretending like you're actually going to shoot me?" At least I'm hoping like hell she's not going to shoot me.

"What makes you so sure that I won't?"

"Because it doesn't make sense to shoot the guy who gave you the best orgasms of your life. The guy who's here to give you another night full of 'em." I smirk at her. Fuck, I want to reach out and drag her against me. My cock is so fucking ready to come out and play.

She smiles and I think she's on board with the idea of letting me in, both into her house and into her body. And then I see her finger pull back, her hand shifts slightly, and the sound of the gunshot blasts through my ears.

I close the distance between us and dislodge the pistol from her hand within seconds. "You just fucking shot at me," I growl, a little dumbfounded that she actually did it.

"I shot near you. Not at you. That was a warning shot. The next one won't be. Get out of my house, Marcel," Zoe grits out between clenched teeth while keeping her eyes on the gun that's now in *my* hand.

I follow her line of sight before setting the pistol on the ground and kicking it across the floor. Then I wrap an arm around her waist and pull her against me while my lips graze her neck. "You don't really want me to leave, do you, Zoe? You and I both know you want me to stay. You want a repeat of that night just as much as I do."

Zoe's head shakes. "No, I don't." Her hands lean on my chest and she pushes me back. Or tries to anyway. I'm not letting go of her that easily. And then something shifts. I can feel it instantly.

Zoe's entire body freezes. She literally shrinks in on herself. Her legs buckle and her knees give out on her. If I wasn't holding her right now, she'd be on the ground. It's not just her body language that tells me something is glaringly wrong. It's the ear-piercing scream she lets out that has me taking a step back. I wait until I know she's steady on her feet before I release her and drop my arms though. I don't want to, but something tells me I need to.

"What's wrong?" I ask her.

Zoe's eyes glaze over. Her face is ashen. She continues to shuffle back until her body hits a wall. She's not looking at me. She's looking past me. Through me.

"Zoe, what's happening?" I keep my tone even. Calm. While maintaining my distance. I don't want her to feel cornered right now.

She's scared. Whatever's happening, she's fucking terrified and I'm praying it's not of me.

"No. No, no, no, not again," she chants over and over as her body sinks to the floor.

"Zoe, I want to help you but I can't do that if you don't tell me what's happening." I crouch down in front of her, slowly moving forward on my knees. I have a feeling I know what she's talking about, but I hope that I'm fucking wrong...

Her eyes focus on me and she frowns. "I can't. I can't do this."

"Do what?" I ask her. "What did I do?"

"You shouldn't be here." Her voice is barely a whisper.

"I am here, though, and I'm not leaving you like this," I tell her. "I want to help you. Tell me what to do."

"I need my phone... Where's my phone?" Her eyes flick around but she doesn't move.

"Where'd you have it last?"

Zoe points to a room behind me. I push up to my feet and walk that way. I find her phone on a coffee table. I swipe it up and rush back to where she's still sitting on the floor in the foyer.

The gun's not far, so I reach out and pick it up before going back to Zoe and handing her both items.

She looks at me inquisitively. "Why are you giving me this?"

"Because you're afraid, and I don't fucking like it," I tell her.

Zoe looks down at her phone and then at the gun. I don't know what she's thinking. What has her this fucking scared. I also don't know why I care so much. That last one is the one that bothers me the most. I don't know this girl. Other than the fact I know how good her pussy feels around my cock.

"I usually call Izzy when I feel like this. She helps," Zoe says.

"Okay, call her."

"I don't think I need to." She peers up at me. No matter how small and unthreatening I try to make myself, she's still so fucking tiny.

"Why?" I ask her.

"You're not... You're not going to hurt me."

"No, I'm not. I will never do anything you don't want me to do, Zoe. I'm not that guy." Though I would love to know the name of *that guy*. The one who hurt her. Because it's evident that someone has.

Chapter Six

H e's not *that guy*. I know that, right? I'm certain that he isn't. He did let go. He's not forcing me to do anything. That's not what has me wanting to take him up on the offer he brought to my door, though. It's the way he's looking at me right now.

Or should I say the way he's *not* looking at me?

He doesn't have that same look Flynn used to have whenever I had an... episode. Marcel doesn't appear disgusted. He also doesn't seem to be searching for a way out.

When I pushed on his chest and he didn't let go, I was taken back to a time I'd do anything to never remember. I can't control when the flashbacks come on, and I can't stop them once they start. But Marcel stayed. He could have easily gotten up and left. He doesn't owe me anything.

Flynn did that a few times. Just left me in the midst of a panic attack, his logic being that he thought I needed space. I didn't. I needed help. Understanding. Patience. But I would never admit that to him.

Marcel doesn't appear to be in a rush to leave. And he gave me my gun back. Just handed it to me like it was nothing. With that one gesture, he made me feel like I had control. I'm not an idiot. I know he could easily overpower me and take it back if he wanted to.

"Why didn't you leave?" I ask him.

"Why would I leave you when you clearly need help?"

I lift a shoulder. "You don't know me."

"Maybe not, but I'm also not an asshole. I'm not

going to just leave you alone if you're panicked or scared."

I raise an eyebrow at him. "You are an asshole."

"I deserve that." He smiles. "You're right. I'm usually an asshole with brief moments of good behaviour between."

I can't help but smile back at him. What is it about this guy that makes me feel so much more at ease? I don't think I've ever recovered from a flashback so quickly before. They can last for ages and I'm left a mess afterwards. But, somehow, Marcel has me smiling.

Something comes over me at that realisation, and I leap up and throw myself at him. Straddling his lap before my lips connect with his. I wrap my arms around his neck and hold him tight to me. There's this hunger inside me I'm not sure I've ever felt, and it's for him.

Marcel's hands roam up and down my back. Grabbing hold of my ass, he pulls my core against the hardness of his cock. I moan into his mouth. It's not enough. I need more. My hands push down on his shoulders, until his back is flat on the marble floor. Shifting my position on top of him, I undo his belt, then his pants. Then my hand reaches inside and frees his cock. It springs up, hard and leaking precum.

I want to taste it. Leaning forward, I run my tongue along the tip.

"Fuck, Zoe," Marcel groans, pulling my head back to look me in the eye. "Are you sure about this?"

"Am I sure I want you to fuck me all night and give me as many orgasms as you think you're capable of giving me? You should probably try to set a new world record or something, because not only do I want this, Marcel, I need it," I tell him.

"Well then, call the Guinness people, babe, because we're about to break records." He smirks.

"I like your confidence." I grin until a thought comes to mind. "Condom? We need one." Surely, he's one of those guys who carries those things around with him wherever he goes.

He proves that I'm right when he shifts his weight, reaches into his back pocket, and fishes out his wallet. I grab it from his hands, digging through all the cards and cash until I find the foil packet.

"We're probably going to need more than one," I tell him before ripping the packet open. "But it's a start." Then I roll the latex down his length.

Marcel watches me as I stand and slide my panties

along my legs. Before I settle back on top of him, my pussy against his cock. His head tips backwards and his eyes focus on the ceiling as he inhales deeply, his fingers digging into my hips. He's trying to control himself. Which is the last thing I want. I need him to lose control. I need a repeat of that night at the hotel. I don't need him treating me like I might break after what he witnessed.

I want him to need this as much as I do.

When his head shifts in my direction again, and we make eye contact, I can see it. The lust, the desire. "You're going to need an ice pack tomorrow," he grunts.

"Why?" I ask as I grind against his cock.

"Because I'm going to fuck you so hard your vagina's going to bruise. And when it twinges every time you take a step, you'll remember that you're the one who asked for this. You'll remember that I'm the one who made you feel so fucking good."

Before I can respond, Marcel is sitting up. He somehow manages to get to his feet, taking me with him. My legs wrap around his waist as he starts walking. A few seconds later, he is lowering me onto the sofa and lining up his cock with my entrance. Marcel lifts one of my legs, kissing my ankle before resting it on his shoulder. His body leans over mine, bending me like a damn pretzel as he pushes into me.

He stills when his eyes connect with mine. "Remember: you can ask me to stop at any point and I will."

"Thank you." My voice is hoarse, the emotions he's bringing to the surface foreign, and I'm not a hundred percent sure I want to feel them right now. Which is why I'm grateful when he starts moving.

Marcel pumps in and out of me, slowly at first. And then his fingertips dig into my hips, holding me in place as he picks up speed. His cock slamming into me relentlessly, hitting some spot deep inside that has me seeing the damn stars. I'm reduced to a screaming, wet mess as he fucks me. Right now, the entire world could go up in flames and I wouldn't stop him. Stop this.

Like I said, I need this. I'm prepared to burn if it means reaching that earth-shattering orgasm I can feel building within me.

"Fuck, you feel good. The way your cunt is choking my cock right now... Fuck, Zoe. I could get lost in your pussy and never look for a way out," Marcel grunts through his thrusts.

"Shit! Oh, fuck!" I bite down on my bottom lip.

"That's it. Light up for me, babe. Come all over my cock." He covers my mouth with his, swallowing my screams.

And like he flipped a switch, my entire body is alight with pleasure as my orgasm crashes over me. Every nerve ending tingling. I lose track of everything but that pleasure. How good it feels. It's addictive. I haven't had it a lot and I already know I don't want to go another lifetime without it.

I open my eyes, as I'm coming down from my high, to find Marcel staring down at me. When did he stop kissing me?

"So fucking pretty," he says. His thrusts have slowed, his movements almost reverent. "I love watching you come."

I'm sure if my cheeks weren't red before, they would be now. His attention is a lot to digest. How can a stranger make you feel like you're the most important thing in the world with just a look? Or am I that desperate for love that I'm making shit up in my head?

Who knows? What I do know, is how much I like the way Marcel feels buried inside me. That's what I need to focus on. Nothing else matters right now.

"Where's your bedroom?" he asks.

"Upstairs." Before the word is out of my mouth, Marcel is picking me up, somehow managing to keep me impaled on his dick as he does.

He walks through my house, as if he's memorised

the floor plan, heading straight up the stairs and into my bedroom. I should be concerned that he opened the door without being told which one it is. But then I feel his cock move inside me and all common sense is gone. I expect my back to hit the mattress, but Marcel spins around and falls backwards, pulling me down on top of him as he goes.

"Ride me. Take control, babe. Show me how much you love my dick buried inside your dripping wet cunt." His hands pull the bottom of my dress up and over my head, revealing my body to him.

Cupping my breasts, he rolls each nipple through the tips of his fingers as I start to move up and down on his shaft. He wasn't wrong. I do love having him inside me. It feels different in this position. Deeper. Every time I bottom out, my clit grinds on his pelvis and sends shots of pleasure through me.

"That's it. You're so good, Zoe. So fucking good," Marcel grits out, his jaw tight as his abs flex underneath my hands.

"I... oh god!" I can feel another orgasm building. How can I be ready to come again so soon?

"Good girl, Zoe, you're doing great. Show me. I want to see you make yourself come on my cock. Use me to make yourself feel good," he says.

And I do. I ride him as if my life depends on it.

With one thought on my mind. Coming. I move in any way that makes me feel good. Chasing that feeling all the way to the end. Grabbing on and holding firm.

"Fuck yes," Marcel groans as my body tightens and I explode.

I know I scream. I can't make out the words though. The sounds Marcel makes, that's what I focus on. I've never heard anything so good in my life. Hearing him lose control, hearing him come because of me, it's a turn on like nothing else.

The sun streams in through the windows. I must have left the curtains open last night. It's the only reason I'd wake up this early on a weekend. My body aches as I roll over, and my hand lands on something next to me. Which has my eyes springing open.

"Shit," I hiss. Everything I did last night plays back at twice the speed in my brain. My lips spread into a smile before I force them to stop. Reaching out a hand, I shake Marcel's shoulder. "Get up!"

"Huh?" He tries to grab my wrist. I scoot back and climb out of the bed.

"Get up. Your time here has expired. I got shit to do, and you're not it. Sorry, sweetheart, but you have to leave." I throw his words back at him. Though I must say my delivery was much nicer.

"You have to be kidding me. Really, Zoe?" He glares at me.

"*Really,* Marcel. You need to leave."

To my surprise, he gets out of the bed with a smirk on his face. I watch as he disappears through my adjoining bathroom, closing the door behind him. Then the water starts running. And the image of that man naked in my shower starts playing in my head. I can't deny how tempting it is, the thought of going in there with him. I'm about to cave into that temptation when my phone vibrates on the bedside table. I frown. I don't remember bringing it upstairs.

But there it is, plugged into a charger and all. Did Marcel do that for me? If so, why?

Seeing Mikhail's name on the screen stops my wondering and has me hitting answer instead. "Hello."

"Zoe? How are you?" The Russian accent and the genuine concern I hear in his voice make me homesick. I really do need to visit New York soon.

"I'm great. How are you? How're the babies?"

"Who's the guy, Zoe?" Mikhail asks.

"What guy?" I play dumb, even though I know it's pointless. He wouldn't be asking if he didn't already know.

"The one who showed up to your house last night and didn't leave?" Mikhail clarifies. "You can either tell me, or I can send some friends over now to find out."

"I'm fine, Mikhail. He's just a friend. That's all."

"Are you really okay? You'd tell me if you weren't, right?"

"You'd be the first person I'd call. Well, the second, after Izzy. But only because she'd kill the both of us if I didn't call her first." I laugh, trying to lighten the mood.

"I want you to have freedom, Zoe. I do. And I want you to be a young adult, but I also want you to be safe. And choose who you spend time with wisely," he says.

"I'm being careful. I promise."

Mikhail sighs into the phone but seems to drop the subject. "Okay. Should I send the jet to bring you home for a weekend soon?"

"I'd like that, but let me look at my work schedule and get back to you."

"Anytime, Zoe," he says.

"I know."

"I love you," he tells me in Russian.

"Love you too," I say right as the door to the bathroom opens. "I have to go. I'll call you back later." I cut the call without hearing whatever else Mikhail was going to say. I can only imagine the surprise on his face. No one hangs up on Mikhail Petrov. Except maybe his wife. And now me.

Marcel stands in the doorway of my bathroom, nothing but a white towel wrapped around his waist. There's a look I can't decipher on his face. Without a word, he snaps out of whatever trance was holding him captive. Then he walks over to his discarded clothes and gets dressed. Which takes him less than five minutes to do.

He takes a few steps in my direction, his hands tucked into his pockets as he approaches me. "Last night was fun."

"It was."

Then Marcel leans down and kisses my forehead. "See you around, Zoe," he says before turning around and walking out.

"What the hell was that?" I whisper the question to the now-empty room.

Chapter Seven

I've been watching her all day. Well, technically, I've been waiting for her to finish work all day. Instead of letting her know I'm here, waiting for her, I'm following her down the streets of Melbourne. Wondering where she's going. I stop when she enters a building.

A building I know all too well. What I don't

know is why someone like Zoe would be going in there. It's a strip club, owned by the Bratva. I shouldn't fucking be here. We're not exactly on friendly terms with that crew.

I can't walk away now, though. Not when Zoe is in there. I need to find out why. Because if she's on that stage, I will drag her ass off it. Kicking and screaming if I have to. My stomach twists at the thought of her being gawked at by the sleazy fuckers who hang out in that club.

It takes less than two minutes after I walk through the door to draw the attention of the men I would have preferred to avoid. "What the fuck are you doing in our club, De Bellis?"

"Looking for someone. A woman, about yay high." I hold up my hand just below my shoulder. "Blonde, American. You see her?" I ask the two angry-looking Russians.

The moment I mentioned American, their demeanours changed completely. They went from annoyed to downright lethal. Guess they know exactly the girl I'm looking for. Then I make the mistake of taking my eyes off them to look through the dimly lit space.

That's when the first hit comes. A fist slams into my jaw, jarring my head backwards. I duck the next one, but then a third gets me in the ribs. I start throwing back, focusing on the fucker in front of me. Until I'm grabbed from behind. My arms held down.

"Fuck you. Fight like a fucking man, cocksucker," I hiss out while spitting blood from my split lip.

"You're asking questions about a woman you shouldn't even know exists. You'd be smart to forget her," the guy says in a thick Russian accent.

"Yeah, and you'd be smart to remember who the fuck I am," I growl at him. I kick out a leg, managing to swipe his out from under him. Throwing my head back, I connect with the second fucker's face. I hear the sound of crunching bone and smile. His arms drop, but before I can do anything about it, the first guy is back up and laying into me. This, of course, gives the one behind me time to recover.

Two on one, seems fair. Assholes know I'm alone. I don't give a fuck, though. I won't go down easy. They want to try to take me out, they're going to have to work up one hell of a sweat.

For every punch I manage to block, or deliver, I'm hit with two. And by the time my ass is being carried out of the club, I'm fucked. My entire body black and blue and bleeding. I can feel bruises forming on top of fucking bruises. I could call one of my brothers to come and pick me up, but they'd want answers I don't want to give them yet.

I pull out my phone out and text Dom.

ME:

I need you to come get me.

I attach a Google maps location to my message.

DOM:

I'm not a fucking Uber.

ME:

Bring a towel, unless you want blood on your fancy leather seats.

The little dots tell me that he's reading the message. His bullshit about him not being an Uber was just that. Bullshit. I know he'll come and get me.

DOM:

Be there in five. If you bleed on my seats, you're buying the car.

I laugh and then stop and pocket my phone when my eyes flick back to the building. I consider going back in there. I never did see Zoe. But then she walks out the door and starts down the street in the opposite direction. I know she's connected to the Bratva. That doesn't mean I have to like it. But seeing her walk into that club just made me realise how connected she really is.

I don't care who her parents or *adoptive* parents are. I don't give a fuck about that. Something happened to that woman and I want to know what it was.

I've been trying to dig into it all day, and I keep coming up empty. Zoe Petrov is an alias, and there are no records of whoever she was before that.

When I see the pretentious Rolls Royce roll to a stop in front of me, the number plates reading MCKINLEY in gaudy lettering, I push off the wall and gingerly approach the kerb.

The door opens from the inside, and I fall into the seat. "What the fuck happened to you?" Dom grunts.

"Careful, Dominic, you're going to make me think you actually care about me." I laugh, stopping short when my entire body hurts from the movement.

"It's mere curiosity, asshole. There's no caring involved," he says. "Where am I taking you?"

"Home," I groan.

It takes five minutes of driving in silence before Dom speaks up again. He eyes me from his peripheral. "You went after Zoe, didn't you?" When I don't answer him, he laughs. "Of course you did. You've no sense of self-preservation."

"I'm alive, aren't I?" I counter.

"Barely. I've fed people more alive than you to my pigs, Marcel."

I shiver at the thought. Creepy fuckers, they are. Dominic has a farm a few hours out of town. It's how he disposes of people who need disposing of. He doesn't do it because he needs to. He could easily outsource his dirty work. Dominic is the heir to the McKinley family's billion-dollar empire. But the crazy fucker enjoys feeding his pets. Guy definitely has more than a few screws loose.

"I know you don't want it, but you're getting it anyway," Dom says out of nowhere.

"Getting what?"

"My advice. Dipshit." He pauses and looks across at me. "If it's not serious, like for the rest of your life type of serious, leave her alone."

The glare I send Dom does nothing to wipe the smirk off his face. "Not all of us are the forever type, Dom."

"Like I said, then leave her alone. That girl has gone through enough without getting mixed up in your family's drama."

"What does that mean? What has she gone

through?" I shift in my seat to face him. As painful as it is, he has my full attention now.

Dom doesn't answer me and I don't push him for more. When he pulls into the driveway of my house, I turn to him again. "Thanks for the ride. And the advice," I tell him.

"So you're actually going to listen to me and stay away from Zoe?" Dom tilts his head at me.

"I didn't say that." I slide out of the car and slam the door before he can reply.

I enter the house and make it as far as the first step before Gio confronts me. "What the fuck happened to you?"

"You should see the other guy." I laugh. I try to brush past him, but my big brother ain't having it.

Gio places a hand on my shoulder, turning me around. "Follow me," he demands before stepping in front of me. The thing is, he's not just my older brother. He's also the Don of the family, which means if he tells me to follow, I really don't have an option.

Gio heads into the games room, where I fall onto the sofa, lean my head back on the top of the frame, and close my eyes. I really just want to jump in the shower and collapse into bed. Maybe sleep for a few days.

Gio fills a glass with Cinque, without bothering to pour me one. As if on cue, or more likely they've been summoned, two of my brothers walk into the room. Look at me and stop.

"What the fuck?" Santo asks. I shake my head. There's no point telling them the story until Gabe arrives because I know Gio's called them all here.

The doc is the next one to come through the door. He doesn't ask questions, just sets his bag down at my feet and gets to work patching me up.

"What the fuck happened?" Gabe growls when he enters the room a few minutes later.

"You should see the other guys," I repeat. And once again, no one appreciates my humour. These fuckers really need to learn how to take a joke.

They're all staring at me. I get it. I've looked better.

I hiss when the doc presses on my chest and lower abdomen. "I don't need an x-ray to tell me there's at least one cracked rib," he says.

"Yeah, figured. Hurts like a fucking bitch," I grit out between clenched teeth. My fists clench as I embrace the pain.

Gabe pours himself a whiskey, and again, no one fucking bothers to get me one.

"Just stitch me up, Doc. I gotta get back out

there and find those fucking assholes," I grunt. I was planning on doing that tomorrow, after I've recovered a little. But now, my anger is building, and I want to find them and put a bullet between their eyes.

"You should take a few days, at the very least, to recover," Doc says.

About twenty minutes later, the doc finally packs up. He hands me a bottle of pain pills and tells me to chill the fuck out. That's not fucking happening, though.

As soon as the doc is out of the room, I push myself off the sofa and onto my feet. "I'm going to fucking kill them all," I hiss through the pain.

"Who?" Gio asks.

"The fucking Russians," I yell out.

"The Russians jumped you?" Gabe asks with a raised brow. We're not on friendly terms with them, but we don't just start fights with each other either.

"Yes," I tell him.

"Where were you?" Gio pins me with that look, the one that would have most men pissing their pants.

I break eye contact first, walk over to the bar, and pick up a bottle of Cinque. Pulling out two of the pain pills the doc gave me and washing them down with the whiskey before turning back to my brother. "It doesn't matter where I was."

"Actually it does. Where were you, Marcello?" Gio repeats.

I feel four sets of eyes on me. "I was at Varka," I admit.

"Why the fuck were you at a Russian club?" Gabe asks.

I shrug a shoulder. And immediately regret it. Shit hurts. "Looking for someone."

"You'll do nothing to retaliate. You shouldn't have been there. You're lucky they left you fucking breathing. Whoever she is, she's not worth this," Gio says while gesturing a hand towards my face.

"I agree with him. No chick is worth... *that*," Santo spits.

"Why?" This comes from Gabe.

"What do you mean why?"

"Why were you looking for someone in a Russian club?" he clarifies.

"It doesn't matter." I fall back onto the sofa.

"Well, I'd love to stay and chat but I got shit to do," Vin says before walking out of the room.

"Did you talk to him?" I direct to Gabe while jutting my chin towards where our baby brother was just standing. I could use a quick shift in topic. And truth is, he needs their attention a hell of a lot more than I do. Especially after what we found at one of the properties only Vin seemed to know about. The shit inside those walls was the thing of nightmares.

"I did." Gabe nods.

"And?"

"And nothing. Who's the girl?" Gabe mimics Gio's glare.

"Zoe," I say. "I met her the night of Santo's bucks." I look to Santo and see how he flinches. The pain is still fresh and I really don't want to send my brother over the deep end.

"Why were you looking for her in a Russian club? Is she Russian? Because if she is, that isn't going to end well for anyone," Gabe questions.

"She's not Russian. She's American," I tell him. "I think she has connections to them, though. Haven't figured out what it is yet. I've been looking for her ever since that night."

It won't take my brothers long to figure out that I'm lying. That I know exactly how she's connected to the Russians and the Bratva. Through their Pakhan. Right now, I'm just trying to buy myself some time. So that I can keep digging into her past. And I can't do that if Gabe knows she's connected to the Petrovs.

"Have you got any more to go on than a first name?" he asks.

"A picture." If there's something to be found, Gabe is usually the one to do it. But it's not her name I need. It's her past.

"Send it to me. I'll find out who she is," he says. "Why wouldn't you just come to me?" My brother sounds almost offended. And now, I feel like shit holding back information. I don't usually lie to my brothers. But something about this girl is different. And I'm not ready to share her or risk them trying to stop me.

"If I don't find her by the end of the week, I'll let you do your thing. But this." I gesture a hand around my face. "Is going to draw her out." I smirk. I'm not stupid. I know my brother. Which means I also know he's going to start looking as soon as he walks out of this room. Curiosity always gets the better of him.

"You got the shit beat out of you to draw her out of hiding?" Gabe asks. "That's the stupidest fucking thing I've ever heard."

"No stupider than fucking one of El's friends. She's going to rip your balls off when she finds out." I laugh at him, figuring now is as good a time as any to mention the fact that I caught him balls-deep in one of Gio's girlfriend's friends. "The house isn't soundproof. I saw you two going at it in the kitchen. Word of advice? If you're trying to keep it under wraps, stop with the sex in public places."

"The kitchen is not a fucking public place, and I'm not fucking her. It was a onetime thing. No one else needs to find out, Marcel," Gabe grinds out.

"Your secrets are safe with me," I tell him while offering a sarcastic two-finger salute.

Chapter Eight

Five days. That's how long it's been since Marcel turned up at my house and delivered on his promise to give me a night of pleasure I'd never forget. Five days I've been wondering if he'll show up again. And then wondering *if* I wanted him to show up again.

My vagina wants him to. That much is evident

by the wetness I can feel every time I think of what Marcel did the other night. And the time before that. The man is skilled, and then I question how a person gets that skilled at sex...

Practice, clearly. Those thoughts lead to an irrational jealousy.

"Earth to Zoe. You in there?" Lucy snaps her fingers at me.

Shaking all thoughts of Marcel from my head, or at least trying to, I give her my full attention. "Sorry. I zoned out," I admit with a shy curl of my lips.

"What's on your mind? Or should the question be who is on your mind?" Lucy lifts an eyebrow at me.

I debate telling her. Marcel is one of her fiancée's friends after all. And I don't want to make things complicated between us or difficult for her. Lucy might be my friend, but she's also my boss. I work for her and Savannah Valentino. The latter of whom I know from my time in New York. When Savannah found out I was looking into moving away, she offered me a position here. I hope to one day be as talented as both Lucy and Savannah are and have my own company. Right now, I'm content with just learning from them, though.

"Is it because your Russian friends beat the crap out of Marcel?" Lucy asks when I don't answer her.

My eyes widen and I can't hold back my gasp. "What?"

"Oh shit, you didn't know?"

"No, what happened? Is he okay?" I rush out. I'm about to pull out my phone and call him. Except I realise I don't have his number.

"He went into Varka, looking for you. Dom had to go and pick him up. Said he'd had the crap beaten out of him. I figured you knew," Lucy says.

"When did this happen?" I ask her.

"A few days ago. I'm sorry. I would have said something earlier..."

"It's okay. How... Where... Do you know where he is right now?" I start clearing off my desk and packing up my things. I probably shouldn't leave in the middle of a meeting, but I need to see him. I need to make sure he's okay, and that he knows I had nothing to do with what happened to him.

"Hold on. Give me a minute." Lucy grabs her phone and brings it to her ear, dialling out to someone. "Dom, where is Marcel right now?" she asks. I don't hear the response, but I do see her roll her eyes. "Stop being so dramatic and just tell me where he is, Dominic McKinley." She waits again and then she laughs. "Don't do that. It's not for me. Zoe wants to know."

Don't do what?

I've heard rumours about Dominic and just how psychotic he can be. All from Izzy, of course. And if that woman is telling me someone else is cray-cray, then I believe her. Because she's probably the most lethal and ruthless person I've ever met. I think she's even more terrifying than Mikhail. When you get on her bad side. Lucky for me, I've only ever seen the good parts of her directed my way.

"Okay, thanks. Love you," Lucy cuts the call. "He's on campus. Let's go. I'll take you there," she offers.

"You don't have to do that." I feel bad enough that I'm leaving while we were in the middle of something.

"I know I don't have to. I want to. It's what friends do, Zoe. Besides, you don't know your way around the uni."

She's right. I don't know my way around that campus. I've never even been there. I'd never find him myself. So I follow Lucy outside and over to her car.

Lucy points to a building. "He'll be coming out of there in about five minutes," she says. "You want me to wait around with you?"

"No, it's okay," I tell her. It'd be better if she didn't. He might not want to see me, and I don't need anyone else to witness my embarrassment. I honestly wouldn't blame him if he turned me away. He got hurt because of me.

"Okay. Call me if you need me for anything," Lucy says.

"I will. Thank you." I hug her before she leaves and then sit down on the bench and wait.

My eyes stay focused on the door Lucy pointed to. This would be the perfect place to people watch. There are students everywhere, but I stay hyperfocused on that door. My heart picks up when the door opens and a crowd starts piling out of the building.

Will I even be able to spot Marcel?

As soon as the question pops into my head, he appears. I mean, how could you not spot him? Besides the fact that the crowd literally parts for him when he walks through. Everyone giving him a wide berth.

Standing up, I lift my bag onto my shoulder, my fingers tight around the strap. That's when his eyes connect with mine. He looks shocked for a split-second before he masks whatever he's thinking.

My eyes burn with tears that want to fall. I know Lucy said he was beaten up, but seeing his face, covered in healing bruises and cuts, I just... I don't like it. I fall back onto the bench. I shouldn't have come here. If he got hurt like that because of me, then I should stay far away from him.

Marcel doesn't drop his intense glare as he heads in my direction, stopping right in front of me. "You okay?" he asks, squatting down so that his face is level with mine.

"I came here to ask you that," I tell him. My hand lifts, wanting to touch his face. I force myself to put it down.

"Why?"

"What happened?" I ask, instead of answering him.

"I ran into a door?" His response comes out as more of a question.

"No, you didn't."

"I didn't. But I'm fine. This." He points to his face. "Is nothing. I've had far worse."

"I doubt that."

"You didn't know my father. Mean son of a bitch, he was," Marcel tells me with a serious look on his face.

"We both must have struck out in the father department," I say before I realise what I've admitted.

"What do you mean?"

"Nothing. I, uh, I'm sorry about what happened. I didn't know. I just thought you should know that. I didn't tell anyone to do this. And if I'd known what they were going to do, I would have stopped it," I say.

"This isn't your fault, Zoe. I walked into a club I had no business being in," he says.

"You were looking for me. That kinda feels like it's my fault."

"Trust me, it was no one's fault but my own. I'm curious, though. Why were you in a Bratva strip club?" he asks. "I know you're not a stripper, so why else would you be there?"

"What makes you so sure I'm not a stripper?" I mean, I'm not. But how is he so certain I'm not moonlighting as one?

"Because my dick has never gotten hard for a

stripper, and I've seen a lot of 'em. But you, Zoe, you make my dick harder than it's ever been before." He doesn't break eye contact as he tells me this. "That's how I know."

"Sooo, you're going off the hardness of your dick? Seems like a reasonable thing to do," I counter, allowing the sarcasm to drip from my words.

"It's never let me down before." Marcel shrugs.

"Right, well, I'll let you get back to whatever you were doing. I just really needed to tell you that I didn't know." I push up from the bench.

Marcel stands with me. "What are you doing right now?"

"I need to get back to the office."

"I know your boss. She'll be fine if you take some time off. Come with me." Marcel reaches for my hand and starts leading me back towards the building.

"Wait! Where are we going?" I ask, struggling to keep up with his long strides.

Turning his head, he looks at me and slows his pace a bit. "I already told you. When I see you, my dick gets hard."

My entire body heats up. He can't be serious right now. We're in the middle of a college campus. I don't say a single word, though, as I follow him into the building. And I don't protest a single bit when he opens a door and pulls me through it before closing it behind us.

It's not until my back is pressed up against that door, Marcel's hands cupping my face and his lips descending onto mine that I finally speak up.

"Wait." I rest a palm on his chest.

Marcel's hands drop and he takes two steps backwards. His eyes flicker across my face. I know what he's looking for. He's wondering if I'm freaking out again. I'm not. The fact that he instantly stepped back doesn't escape me, though.

"You can't seriously want to do this here?"

"Why not?" he asks.

"There are millions of people around, Marcel. What if someone walks in?"

"Millions is an overstatement, babe. And no one is walking in. We can lock the door if it makes you feel better?"

"What if they hear?" I whisper.

"Let 'em." He shrugs. "I want the fucking world to hear you scream my name when I make you come." His eyes travel up and down my body. "You want me to do that, don't you? You want my cock pressing into that tight little cunt of yours? You want to wrap your legs around my waist as I fuck you up against this door?"

I do want that. Damn it. Am I that transparent? I cast my gaze to the floor. Until Marcel's voice has me looking back up.

"Zoe. Take off your panties."

My eyes widen and I look around. My hands have a mind of their own, though, and they start lifting my skirt. Then I reach underneath and pull my panties down my legs, kicking them off from around my ankles.

Marcel bends down and picks them up, before tucking them in the back pocket of his jeans. "Tell me you want this, Zoe. I need to hear the words."

"I want this."

"What exactly do you want?" He takes one step towards me.

"I want you to fuck me," I tell him and can feel my cheeks heating up.

"Fuck, you're adorable. Fucking hot as shit." He undoes the button of his jeans as he pulls a foil packet from one of his pockets.

"You always carry those around?" I ask while that stupid jealousy pushes to the surface again.

Marcel smirks. "Would you prefer I didn't?"

"No, that's not..." I should have kept my thoughts

to myself. Of course, I'm glad he has them. One of us has to be thinking clearly.

"Zoe, I haven't fucked or even wanted to fuck anyone else since I met you." He closes the distance between us, his cock now sheathed in the condom. "I don't want anyone else. Whatever is happening with us, it's only us," he says, leaning in until his lips press against mine. Then his tongue pushes into my mouth.

I jump, wrapping my legs around his waist and locking my ankles together. My core grinds down against his cock. Marcel swallows my moans as he kisses me in a way that has my head spinning. It's the kind of kiss you see in movies but never expect to actually experience yourself.

Chapter Nine

My body still fucking hurts like a bitch, especially with Zoe wrapped around me. No way in hell am I telling her to get off me, though, and there's fuck all chance of me putting her down either.

Stepping forward, I press her back into the door, holding her up with my hips pushed hard against her. My tongue duels with hers, circling around her mouth. I smile against her lips when she moans. That's exactly what I want to hear.

I want all of her moans. I want her to fucking scream this building down. It won't be long before word gets out around town that Zoe Petrov is mine.

I still. *Where the fuck did that come from?*

Do I want to fuck the girl? Yes, more than anything. Do I want to keep her? I'm not supposed to want to. I'm meant to be fucking her out of my damn system. I can't keep her. Nothing good happens to women who get tangled up with my family.

"What's wrong?" The feel of Zoe's hands pressing against the side of my face breaks me from my thoughts.

I smirk. "Nothing. I was contemplating if I should fuck you up against the door like... this." I grind my cock into her pussy again. "Or if I should take you to that desk and bend you over it."

I can feel her wetness dripping on me. It seems she likes both options. "And what did you decide?" she asks.

"The desk," I tell her, even though the answer's obvious, as I'm already tugging her across the room. I spin her around and push on her back until the front of her body is laid over the desk and her ass is up in the air for me. Then, lifting the fabric of her dress up over her ass, I squeeze the globes. "Definitely the right choice," I grunt while admiring the view of her ass. Her wet pussy. "You sure you want this, Zoe?" I rub the head of my cock against her clit while waiting for her to answer me.

Zoe looks over her shoulder at me. "If you don't fuck me, Marcel, I'm going to explode. I want this."

Lining myself up with her entrance, I slowly slide inside her. When I bottom out, I pause before sliding back out and pushing back in. Keeping my movements purposely slow. Partly because my body fucking hurts, but mostly because I want this to last. Her cunt wrapped around my cock is the best fucking thing I've ever felt.

All week I've been telling myself that I made up how good she feels. I didn't. It's real. She's real and the way she feels is fucking real.

Zoe pushes back against me as I glide inside her again. My hands tighten on her hips, holding her in place. This isn't her show. It's mine. I'm in control. This ain't no diplomacy. I'm running a damn dictatorship, and I'll be the only one to decide how I fuck her.

I make my movements even slower. Softer. Zoe growls—literally growls—as she tries to thrust her hips. She turns to glare at me from over her shoulder again. "Marcel, you're torturing me."

"Babe, this isn't me torturing you. This is me savouring every second I get to spend inside this tight fucking cunt of yours." I pick up my pace, wrapping her ponytail in my fist as I pull her head up off the table while arching her back. "So. Fucking. Good," I growl with each forward drive of my hips.

"Oh god!" Zoe screams. I drop her hair and move my hand around to cover her mouth, muffling the noises coming out of her. As much as I love hearing her scream, I don't need the whole fucking campus to hear her too.

I quicken my thrusts again, driving into her harder. One hand still covering her mouth, my other gripping her hip. I can feel it, my impending orgasm. But I need her to come first. I'll never allow myself to finish before her—that's just ungentlemanly.

"I want you coming all over my cock, Zoe. I need you to come for me," I tell her as I slide my hand from her hip, down to her cunt, before pressing my fingers against her clit.

She's so fucking wet. It only takes a few seconds of circling to make her explode. Her teeth bite down onto my palm. *Fuck.* I don't stop, though. I continue fucking her through her release and then finally allow myself to find mine.

I pull out of her and remove the condom, tying it up before throwing it in the bin next to the desk. After tucking my dick back into my pants, I grab Zoe's limp body and spin her around. My fingers brush the loose strands of her hair out of her face. Her eyes blink open and I'm stuck.

I don't know what it is. But there's a need to take her home and look after her. It's weird. I've never felt like this before, like I've just done wrong by her by fucking her in an empty lecture hall.

"You okay?" I ask as I straighten her skirt over her hips.

"Uh-huh," she says.

"You sure?"

"I'm more than okay." Zoe smiles. "But are you? I came here to see if you were okay, not to... well, you know." Her eyes run up my body, and it's a bloody good thing she can't see the bruising under my shirt.

"I could be on my deathbed and I'd still find the energy to fuck you, babe. Nothing is going to stop me from the kind of heaven you're offering," I tell her.

I watch as Zoe's cheeks flame red. "Okay, well. Now that I know you're good... I'll, uh, I should go," she says, clearly flustered.

"I'll walk you. Where did you park?" I pick up my bag and then hers from the floor, where they were both discarded near the door.

"Lucy dropped me off. I'll just get an Uber back to the office."

"I'll drive you." Taking Zoe's hand in mine, I open the door and walk out. The hallway is practically empty, but Zoe still stares at the ground, avoiding all possible eye contact.

We're not even ten steps away from the building when my name's being called out. I turn around and find Dom charging towards us, Lucy trailing close behind him.

"Zoe? Seriously?" he grunts, stopping just in front of us. "Does Izzy know about this little union of yours?"

"No." Zoe shakes her head.

I look between them. It's on the tip of my tongue to tell Dom to fuck off, but he's her friend. Fuck, he's my friend too. Although that could change quickly if he keeps staring at Zoe like she's done something wrong. I learnt early that there really is no such thing as friends when you run in the circles I do. Everyone is always waiting for the opportunity to stab you in the back.

"You know this isn't going to end well for him."

Dom dips his head towards me. Zoe glances in my direction, and a look of guilt crosses her face.

"Whatever you're thinking, stop," I tell her before directing my attention to Dom. "I'm more than capable of handling myself."

"I'm aware, but you don't know who her family is. I do. And you know, it's a little fucking strange to me but I don't want to see your ass in the ground just yet," Dom admits.

"Aw, mate, I knew there was something still beating in that cold, dead heart of yours." I smile. "Don't worry. I'll be fine," I tell him. "I'd love to stick around and chat and all, but I got better shit to do." I don't let go of Zoe's hand as I pivot back around and start walking away.

"Don't say I didn't warn you, fucker," Dom calls out after me.

Raising my free hand, I hold up my middle finger without missing a step.

I have no idea what's going on in Zoe's head right now. I shouldn't care. I really need to get my shit together. I'm not supposed to get attached to a woman. I can already feel myself not wanting to let go of Zoe, and that's a huge fucking problem.

Zoe doesn't say a single word the whole ride to her

office. She doesn't ask how I knew where she worked when I pull up out front either. Instead, she turns to me with a sadness in her eyes I want to wipe away. "I'm sorry. I shouldn't have started this. With you. I never thought you'd get hurt because of me. And I won't be the reason anything else happens to you."

I lean forward and press my lips against hers, holding the back of her head to keep her close to me. "I didn't get hurt because of you. And nothing is going to happen. Trust me."

"You don't know that. My family, they're... protective. Mikhail isn't going to approve of this."

"You know, I'm the one who's meant to be warning you away from me because of who my family is. Because of our curse. And I can't find it within myself to end this, or try to scare you off."

"What do you mean *curse*?" Zoe raises her brows at me.

"My family is cursed. Love never ends well for us, for the women who end up falling for a De Bellis anyway."

"Wait... You actually believe that? That you're cursed?" Zoe's lips tip up into a smile.

"Can't deny cold hard facts, babe." I lift one shoulder.

"Okay, well, I don't believe in curses. But that's beside the point of this conversation."

"Then what *is* the point?"

"That we shouldn't be doing this. Whatever this is," she says.

"We shouldn't. But we're going to do it anyway." I lean in and press my mouth to hers again. My tongue slides through the seam of her slightly parted lips. She opens wider for me, granting me the access to the part of her I desperately want to taste.

Zoe moans as her tongue swirls around mine. Then she breaks the kiss and opens her eyes. "I think we're doing this anyway." She smiles. "But I really do need to get back to work."

"I'll call you later," I tell her as she gets out of the car. Then I wait for her to walk into her office building before I drive away. "What the fuck are you doing? You know better," I ask aloud, to no one but myself.

Chapter Ten

I don't know why I'm so nervous. I've talked to Izzy and Mikhail about a guy before. They both met my last boyfriend. Well, my first and only boyfriend. And Marcel *isn't* my boyfriend. I don't know what he is, but I do know that I don't want to give him up just yet.

He doesn't look at me like I'm broken, even

though I know I am. He doesn't look at me like I'm a project that needs to be fixed or something he's ashamed of. When Marcel looks at me, all I see is desire. He wants me, despite my sharp edges and shattered parts.

He hasn't exactly seen the worst of it yet, but he's not stupid. He knows something happened to me. The way he gives me space when he knows I need it, and then how he just seems to know when I don't. The way he handles my body when we're... intimate. It's a kind of sex I never thought I could possibly like. With Flynn, it was always gentle, slow. Almost as if he was terrified of making me upset. I liked it. I thought it was what I needed.

Or maybe it's not how the sex is at all. Maybe it's the man himself. Marcel is everything I don't want in a boyfriend, and at the same time, he's everything I want right now. My head is so confused. Maybe I shouldn't talk to Izzy about him yet. I mean, it's not even anything serious.

As if the woman has some psychic power, my adoptive mother's name pops up on my phone, causing the device to dance around the kitchen counter. I've been pacing for an hour, debating whether or not to call her, and here she is.

Picking the phone up, I swipe the green answer symbol and bring it to my ear. "Hey."

"Hey yourself. How're things?" Izzy asks.

"Good, hot."

"You could always come home. It's not hot here," she reminds me.

"I think I like someone and I think it's someone you're not going to like, but I really like him and now I don't know what to do," I blurt out in one long rush of words.

"Whoa, slow down and take a breath," Izzy says. "You good?"

"Mhmm," I mumble.

"Okay, start at the beginning. Who is this someone you like that I'm not going to like?"

"It's the guy, the one I met that night I went out," I tell her.

"That was a few weeks ago. You met him again? How?"

"Ah, well, funny thing actually. He's a friend of Dominic and Lucy's..."

"Dom knows this guy?" Izzy questions.

"Uh-huh. They're friends," I reiterate.

"Okay, we both know Dominic doesn't have any friends. But let's pretend this guy of yours *is* friends with Dom. Continue. What's going on?"

"We've met up a few times. That's it really. But I think I really like him, Izzy."

"So, what's the problem? I'm assuming if you're going back for seconds or thirds, he's not a dud in the bedroom."

"No, he's really not. He's... Well, he's really good." I laugh.

"Okay. And what's his name?"

"First, did you know that some of Mikhail's contacts beat him up five days ago?" I ask instead of answering her.

"Why would I know that? I don't even know who this mystery guy is. What'd he do that deserved him getting beat up?"

"He followed me into the club. He's... ah... not exactly on friendly terms with the local Russians."

"Why?"

"I don't know. I didn't ask. Anyway, he's really nice to me, Iz. He doesn't look at me like I'm broken. He's seen me when I haven't been at my best, and he didn't appear fazed at all. He listened. He just seems to get me without judgement."

"You really like him." It's not a question.

"I think I do."

"You still haven't told me his name, Zoe."

"His name's Marcel—Marcello," I say while purposely leaving out his last name.

"He's Italian?" Izzy asks.

"Uh-huh."

"What's his last name?"

"De Bellis," I reply in a much quieter tone.

"Marcello De Bellis. Hot name," she muses.

"Suits him."

"You know the De Bellis family isn't on the up-and-up, Zoe. I don't know all of what they're involved in but I do know it's some shady shit."

"How shady?" I ask her.

"Underworld shit. The same underworld shit that you wanted to get away from, remember?"

"I wanted to get away from New York, not from you and Mikhail. I love you guys. I appreciate everything you've done for me. I don't... Well, I wouldn't be here if it weren't for you." I wipe the stray tear from my eye.

"We love you too, Zoe. You're family. It doesn't matter if you're halfway across the world. You are still family."

"Thank you."

"So tell me more about this Marcel guy. Like, how old is he?"

"He's... around my age. He's in college."

"What's he studying?"

"Business," I tell her.

"Figures." Izzy snorts. "And the sex? You're enjoying it?"

"It's different, mind-blowing. I didn't know sex could be like this, Izzy. I feel safe with him. Like... It sounds stupid, I know, but he makes me feel safe."

"That's not stupid. If you like him and he's treating you well, then I'm sure we will like him too," she says.

"Mikhail's friends beat him up, Izzy."

"He knew what he was doing walking into a Russian club."

"But I didn't even know he was there. I didn't know he followed me, and really, all he did was ask for me."

"Then Mikhail's contacts did their job. Protecting you is important to him. You know that."

"I don't want him getting hurt again because of me."

"I'll talk to Mikhail," Izzy says. "We want you to be happy, Zoe, but I also want you to be safe."

"I know. And I am being safe. Promise." I pause. "Iz, do you believe in curses? Like, is it an Italian thing?"

"A lot of Italians believe in curses. Why do you ask?"

"Just something Marcel said. It's nothing. I just don't think I believe it, you know?"

"Yeah, I get it." There's some shuffling in the background. "Crap, I gotta go. Baby just woke up. Sorry, Zoe," she rushes out.

"It's okay. I'll talk to you later. Thanks, Iz."

I set my phone back on the counter, then go upstairs and run the bath. I feel a whole lot better after talking to Izzy. She has a way of putting my mind at ease, making me feel like everything is going to work out okay.

It's been like that from the very first moment she found me. Saved me. I didn't think I'd ever escape the hell I was in, but she swooped in like my own personal angel. She didn't have to take me into her home, help me heal and give me the skills I needed to enter the world again. While Mikhail made me realise there are some good men in the world. That not all men are sick bastards and only want to hurt me. The way Mikhail loves Izzy, so openly and unconditionally... that's the kind of love I wanted.

After Flynn, I'd reconciled with myself that love wasn't in the cards for me. I'm okay with that, but maybe I can still have some form of a connection with someone? There's something there with Marcel. I wouldn't call it love, but it's something. I like him. And I like the way he makes me feel.

Once the bath is full, I stick my hand in the water to test it before stripping off and getting in. I let my body sink into the warmth and feel the tension release instantly. Leaning my head back, I close my eyes and the first image that pops into my head is Marcel.

Bending me over that desk. The way he took me exactly how he wanted. My thighs squeeze together, while the memory of just how good he felt inside me has my core quivering with need.

I let my fingers run down my torso, past my belly button. Spreading my legs, I run two fingertips through the lips of my pussy. A moan echoes off the bathroom wall as the image of Marcel, and his filthy words, plays back through my mind. Turning me on more and more.

Dipping my fingers inside myself, I imagine that they're Marcel's. That he's here in the bath with me. That he has my legs spread wide and is thrusting in and out of me.

My thumb circle my clit as I pump my own fingers to the same rhythm I imagine him using. I can feel the orgasm building. It's coming fast and hard. I scream out as my legs clench closed, my pussy convulsing as I come with Marcel's name on my lips.

I open my eyes and glance around the bathroom while a sense of loneliness I don't usually feel hits me. I don't know what it means. I just pleasured myself. It felt good. And now the reality that I'm alone in this big house weighs me down like a ton of bricks.

"Argh, not today," I groan while lifting myself out of the tub. I pull the plug and wrap a towel around my torso. I need to distract myself.

I'm not that girl. The one who needs people. I like being alone. I love it actually. When I'm alone, I can just be me. There's no pretending. No feigned bravery required. It's just me. As I am.

I'm not going to start needing someone else now. Even if the someone I want had the ability to pleasure me in a way I clearly can't do for myself.

Chapter Eleven

If you can't beat 'em, join 'em. That's the motto I've decided to adopt when it comes to Little Miss Zoe Petrov. I can't shake the girl, and believe me I've fucking tried. I've spent the last week telling myself I'd stay away from her while failing to do so at every fucking turn.

Which is why I decided to take a different

approach. I can't stay away from her, and as much as I love fucking her, she's more than a late-night booty call. I need to step up my game and show her that whatever is happening between the two of us is changing direction.

When the door to her building opens, my eyes land on her. It takes her a few seconds before she stops and looks across the road, her gaze landing on where I'm leaning against my car. Pushing off the door, I close the distance, stopping right in front of her. My hand cups the back of her neck as my lips slam down onto hers. My tongue pushes past her lips. She tastes like champagne.

"Drinking on the clock?" I ask, pulling away.

"I just landed a huge client. Lucy and I were celebrating." Zoe smiles up at me.

"Congrats."

"What are you doing here?" she asks.

"We're going on a date," I tell her, gripping her hand in mine. "We can come back for your car later. Let's go."

"Wait... What do you mean a date?"

"A date. You have been on a date before, right?" I ask, then correct myself. "Actually, don't answer that. I really don't want to know about your exes."

"I've been on a date, just not with you." Zoe laughs.

"Well, we're fixing that right now."

"A date. Seriously? Why?" she asks as I open the passenger side door to my car.

"Because I like you and you like me, so we're dating. It's the natural progression of things, babe." As I round the hood, I can feel Zoe's eyes on me. I jump in and glance over at her. "What?"

"What makes you so sure that I like you?" she asks with a huge grin spread out on her face.

"Well, it was only just last night that you were screaming my name and clinging to me like a lifeline." I smirk.

"That was sex. I like sex with you, sure. But that has nothing to do with me liking you as a person."

My hand slaps on my own chest. "Are you telling me you're using me for my body and not my personality?"

"Well, I've gotten to know your body pretty well. Your personality? That's still a stranger to me." Zoe shrugs.

I start the ignition and pull out onto the street. "That's the whole point of dating, Zoe. You get to know each other."

"I guess," she says.

Reaching over the console, I pick up her hand, tangling my fingers with hers before resting our joined palms on my thigh. "What's wrong, babe?"

"Nothing," she says while biting the corner of her lower lip. I can feel her hand begin to tremble in mine.

"Don't bullshit me, Zoe. You don't have to. What's wrong?"

"I just don't think I'm dating material. Maybe we should just keep doing what we've been doing," she suggests.

"What makes you think you're not dating material?" I pivot in my seat to look at her when I pull up at a red light.

"I've tried it before. I wasn't... It's just not a good idea."

"You didn't try it with the right person," I tell her. The thought of her dating anyone else drives an irrational surge of jealousy through me.

Zoe doesn't say anything. Instead, she looks out the window. Away from me. The light turns green and I continue driving. I know she has a lot of insecurities. I'm not an idiot. I also know she's been hurt and is suffering from post-traumatic stress after whatever the fuck happened to her. I haven't asked her what that thing was. Truth is, I'm hoping that with time, she'll feel comfortable opening up to me. I can be patient. I can wait. It's not like I'm walking away from her. It seems I'm incapable of doing that.

I park the car, and Zoe finally turns her face back to me. "Where are we?"

"We're taking dancing classes." I smile at her before jumping out of the car. Her jaw is still hanging open when I reach her door and open it.

"What do you mean dancing classes?" She takes my offered hand.

"We're going to learn ballroom dancing."

"Why?"

"A couple of reasons. One, it's one of the few date ideas I could think of that lets me keep your body pressed up against mine for as long as possible. Two, it'll save us time when we eventually get hitched. My brother and his fiancée are getting married in a few days, and El has Gio practicing their first dance all over the damn house."

"That's... insane. We're not getting married. We're barely even dating, Marcel."

"*Yet.* We're not getting married yet, Zoe. Besides, you never know what the future holds. A lot of marriages started with a couple just like you and me dating."

"Okay, let's learn how to dance. But if I break

your toes—because that's a real possibility—don't say I didn't warn you." She smiles.

I guide Zoe into the studio I booked out before we enter a room full of mirrors. Every wall reflecting an image of us at a different angle. I can't help but imagine just how good it'd be to fuck Zoe in the middle of this room. No matter where I looked, I'd be greeted by the sight of her.

"Are you using dancing as a euphemism for sex, Marcel?" Zoe asks. The twinkle in her eye tells me she's hoping I am.

"No." I laugh, but before I can say more, the door opens and the instructor walks in.

"Mr De Bellis, welcome. And this must be the beautiful Zoe. Welcome, welcome. I'm Travis, your instructor." He waves his arms theatrically.

"Thank you," I say, pulling Zoe's body next to mine while my arm wraps around her waist.

"Okay, first up, we're going to learn the foxtrot, and then we will go from there. Have either of you danced before?" Travis explains as he performs a few steps with his feet.

"No," I lie. I've taken lessons before. Knowing how to conduct one's self in proper company was a requirement that comes with my last name. We were forced to attend a lot of galas. And do you know what they do at those things? Dance.

"No, I haven't," Zoe says, her voice a lot quieter than usual.

"Never fear. We'll have you both whipping around the room with the best of them before long. Shall we begin?" Travis asks.

"Yes, thank you," I answer for us. Then I guide Zoe to stand in front of me, pick up her hand, and place it on top of my shoulder before gripping her other palm in mine.

"I thought you said you haven't done this before," she whispers.

"I've seen movies." I smirk.

Half an hour into the lesson, my feet are throbbing after being impaled by Zoe's heels multiple times, but the last thing I am is a quitter. I know she'll get the hang of it eventually. Until then, I can handle a little pain in my toes.

Then something shifts. I can instantly tell that something isn't right. Zoe's body goes stiff and cold.

Her skin is so cold. I look down at her face and notice that vacant look I've seen before. This isn't Zoe. She's not here. She's trapped in whatever nightmare she's escaped.

I step back, knowing she needs space. I don't ever want to be the reason she's forced to endure one of these attacks from her past. "Zoe? It's okay," I tell her. The instructor pauses the music. I glance in his direction. "Can you give us a minute?"

Travis nods his head and disappears.

I watch as Zoe's body starts slipping to the floor and catch her right before her knees hit the hardwood. Lowering her down, I sit in front of her. "Zoe, it's okay. It's just us, babe. Me and you. No one else."

She doesn't respond. She's staring right through me. "No. Stop. Don't," she cries out, her voice soft and broken.

I have no idea what to fucking do. I need to help her, but this is so far out of my element. Fuck.

"Zoe, please look at me. You're safe here," I tell her. "No one is going to hurt you." Anyone who wants to try to touch her will have to go through me, and I'm not fucking easy to get through.

Zoe's eyes blink rapidly and I can see her coming back. It's slow, but eventually she looks at me with recognition. "Marcel? What happened?" she asks while her eyes bounce around the room. "Oh god. I didn't... I... I'm so sorry." She turns back to me. "I didn't mean to... I don't know..."

"Zoe, stop. It's fine. You're okay. We are okay." I cup her cheeks in my hands and wipe the stray tears away. "It's okay."

"I've embarrassed you. I'm sorry. You did all this. You planned all this and I couldn't do it," she says, keeping her gaze on the floor.

I tilt her face upwards. "No, you didn't embarrass me. And you did do it. We were dancing just fine, Zoe. You haven't done anything wrong."

"You're not mad?"

My brows draw down. "That I just got to dance with the hottest chick in Melbourne for half an hour? What do I have to be mad about?"

"I ruined it," she whispers. "I didn't mean to ruin it."

"You haven't ruined anything, babe. Besides, this is just the start of our date. You didn't think I would take you out and not feed you, did you?" Before she has a chance to answer me, I add, "Come on, what do you say we get out of here? I have a picnic blanket and a basket full of food with our names on it."

"A picnic?" Zoe's lips finally curl into the

makings of a smile. Not quite there yet. But I'll take it.

"A picnic, in the park." I nod.

"Are you sure?"

"I don't think I've ever been more sure of anything in my life." I push to my feet and hold out a hand, pulling her up when she accepts it.

It's on the tip of my tongue to ask her what happened, to find out what triggered her. I don't though. I feel like bringing attention to her panic attack is the last thing she needs right now. So I'll do what I'm good at. I'll mask my feelings, hide the fact that I want to fucking kill whatever bastard hurt her, and I'll give her the best damn date she's ever experienced.

Chapter Twelve

I cannot believe I landed this client. This place is huge. I've seen big, over-the-top homes. But this one is something else. Mr Lobson bought this place a month ago. He's old money, from what I can tell. I still don't know what he actually does. I just know he's in his mid-fifties, has a kind smile, and a nonexistent budget for me to redesign the interior of his newest property.

Lucy lets out a long whistle. "Man, this place is insane. Must be nice to be a member of the one-percenter club, huh," she says.

I side-eye her. "You should know." I laugh.

Lucy comes from old money, one of Australia's wealthiest families in fact. So does her fiancé, and let's just say those two getting married is going to create the next generation of combined wealth for whatever children they decide to have.

"Yeah, but still... this place is amazing," she says while spinning around in a circle.

We're standing in the foyer. There's one of those twin staircases on each side and black-and-white marble flooring as far as the eye can see. The clicks of our heels echo off the walls. The house is completely empty. It's a bare canvass. A designer's dream.

"Where do we even begin?" I ask Lucy.

"Let's just focus on one room at a time. It's going to be a long day, Zoe. I hope you ate your Wheaties this morning," she replies before taking off down the foyer.

Following after her, I try to absorb everything that is this house. Mentally planning colours and styles with each room we pass. "What do you think Mr Lobson does?" I ask Lucy.

"No idea. I've never heard of the Lobsons," she says.

"Don't you think that's a little strange? Like, you know everyone in this city."

"Maybe he's new to town. What I do know is he's paying us a great deal to have this place ready within the next month."

"Right, let's do this." I smile. I always get excited about jobs, but there's just something thrilling about being able to complete a whole house like this. Starting completely from scratch. "I'm going to take a look upstairs. You okay down here?" I ask Lucy.

"Yep, go for it," she says. She has her phone out and is snapping pictures for reference.

Making my way back through the empty house, I walk up the staircase. As beautiful as this property is, it's a little eery. I'm thankful Lucy is working on this project with me. I don't think I'd want to be in this house alone.

When I reach the top of the stairs, I look left and then right. I've seen the floor plans. I know all the rooms on this level. I decide to head for the first bedroom, which is going to be a guest room, so it should be an easy place to start.

I step inside and open the internal doors to the walk-in wardrobe and en-suite bathroom, where I sit on the floor with my back against the wall. Then I pull out my tablet and start working on design concepts for this space.

Half an hour later, I'm jerked out of my zone by the buzzing of my phone. I dig it out of my bag and see Marcel's name pop up on the screen. I push on the notification to open his messages.

MARCEL:

I should have stayed in Melbourne.

ME:

And miss your brother's wedding?

MARCEL:

Better than missing you.

ME:

It's a weekend. You'll survive.

Marcel left last night to go to some tropical paradise island. He'll be back on Monday. It's really not that long to be apart.

MARCEL:

What are you doing?

I snap a picture of the empty room and send it to him.

ME:

Coming up with design ideas.

MARCEL:

What are you doing over the weekend?

ME:

Nothing really. Probably staying in.

MARCEL:

I could have the jet come and get you. Bring you here.

ME:

I don't think we're at the meet-the-family stage yet. Besides, I have laundry to do this weekend.

MARCEL:

You and I both know you have housekeepers, Zoe.

How the hell does he know that?

Technically, Mikhail and Izzy have housekeepers. I'm living in their house. As much as I tried to tell them I didn't need staff, my adoptive parents insist on making my life as easy and carefree as they can.

ME:

I'm washing my hair.

MARCEL:

I could wash it for you. I'd make it... pleasurable.

Damn it. Now I'm thinking about being in a shower with the man. I don't have time to contemplate just how pleasurable Marcel could make things. Not right now anyway. Later tonight, when I'm alone in my bed, that's when I'll revisit the idea.

ME:

I have no doubt. But I'm staying home, and you're enjoying your brother's wedding.

MARCEL:

Expect me at your front door Monday night. You'll be my first stop when I land.

ME:

Okay. Have fun.

I throw my phone back into my purse and continue with the list I was putting together before the interruption.

***

My heels land halfway down the foyer as I kick them off my feet. The thud of my bag falling onto the entry table rings out through my ears. I'm exhausted.

A good kind of exhausted, but exhausted all the same.

"What did those red bottoms do to you?"

I jump ten feet in the air at the sound of the voice, before a squeal escapes me and I'm running towards its owner at lightning speed. "Izzy, oh my god! What, when? How are you here?" I ask, throwing my arms around her neck.

"Just landed an hour ago," she says.

"Why? I mean, not why? But I didn't know you were coming? Where's Mikhail? The kids?" I look around, waiting for the rest of them to appear.

"Mikhail just took them out for ice cream with my dad." Izzy rolls her eyes. "We have about an hour to ourselves before they're back. Which means you have an hour to tell me all about this Marcel fella."

"Fella?" I lift an eyebrow at her, the smile on my face not wanning. I didn't realise how much I've missed her.

"Yeah, *fella*. Follow me. I have a bottle of wine open already and I don't want you to leave out any details."

After two glasses of the good stuff, I start to relax, feeling a light buzz. Something that allows me to start to open up more about Marcel—probably more than I should. "I feel like I shouldn't like the way he... the way we, well, have sex," I tell Izzy.

"What do you mean?"

"It's different from how things were with Flynn. Rougher, I guess."

"Rougher? But you like it?"

I nod my head. "There hasn't been anything Marcel has done with me I don't like," I admit.

"Then don't overthink it. If you like it, he likes it, go with it."

"He took me dancing." I smile.

"Dancing?"

"Mhmm. It was weird at first, and then it wasn't. And then I had a flashback and freaked out a little."

"You didn't call me." Izzy's brows draw down, and I realise her confusion.

"I didn't need to," I say. "Marcel... he just kept talking to me. I don't know how or why, but he didn't seem fazed."

"Okay."

"Flynn used to get embarrassed whenever it happened. Especially if someone else saw me."

"Flynn is a pussy-ass motherfucker," Izzy grunts. "There is nothing to be embarrassed about."

"Marcel says the same thing."

"I think I might like this Marcel guy," she hums thoughtfully, while raising her glass to her lips.

"I don't." Mikhail's voice booms through the room. He's followed in by Mabilia and Little Neo. Then Big Neo, who's holding baby Lex.

"Mikhail, she's happy. Don't you dare ruin it." Izzy glares at her husband.

"I would never do such a thing," Mikhail says as he leans in to kiss her before pressing his lips to my forehead. "Zoe, it's been way too long."

"I know," I tell him. I'm then bombarded by a frenzy of little hands as Mabilia and Neo jump on me, both squealing out my name.

"Okay, give Zoe some space." Izzy scoops up Neo but leaves Mabilia with me.

I love this little girl. She was just a tiny baby when I first went to live with them, and now she's a mini Izzy, right down to the sass and recklessness. "Zoe, I missed you most," Mabilia says.

"I missed you too, so much. Like a whole lot."

"I know," she replies confidently, and I laugh. I wish I had just a tenth of her confidence.

"So, where is this Marcel?" Mikhail asks.

"He's out of town. His brother's getting married," I say, snuggling into Mabilia and peppering her cheeks with kisses.

"And he didn't take you? Sounds like a *neudachnik*," Mikhail grunts.

"A what?"

"A loser," he repeats in English.

"He wanted to take me. I said no," I explain. "Also, he's not a loser." I have this overwhelming need to defend Marcel bubbling in my chest.

"Guess I'll be the judge of that when I meet him." Mikhail shrugs.

"He's good to me. I promise. Please be nice."

"I'm always nice, Zoe."

Izzy snorts from where she's standing beside me. "Yeah, and I'm a saint."

"You've always been a saint in my eyes, *bella*," Big Neo says.

"Thanks, Papa." Izzy beams. She's a big-time daddy's girl if I ever saw one.

"I'm going to go put these two little heathens to bed. Don't go anywhere. We're not done with our conversation," Izzy tells me. She then turns to her father. "Papa, help me drag Mabilia away from Zoe."

Mabilia doesn't let go easily. Her little arms hold on me tight. "I'll come and see you before I go to bed," I promise, and only then does she allow herself to be pried away.

I know Izzy left me alone with Mikhail on

purpose. He has something to say, which is why I wait for him to talk first. It doesn't take long. "Are you happy, Zoe?"

I consider his question, really think about it, before replying, "I am."

"What about his family?" Mikhail asks. "You wanted to get away from the lifestyle, Zoe. Getting involved with a De Bellis isn't just being involved. It's diving right in. It's not safe, *docha*." Mikhail leans forward, his elbows resting on his legs.

"I think that sometimes you don't really get to choose. You know that, Mikhail. I can't help the fact I like him. And maybe the risk of being with him is worth it. I don't know. We're still just getting to know each other."

"I'm going to have a couple of the guys tail you for a bit. I need to know that you're safe, Zoe."

"I don't need people following me. I appreciate it, but it's not necessary. I swear. I'm okay." I know what I say right now doesn't really matter. Mikhail will have his guys watching me anyway. Honestly, I wouldn't be surprised if they always have been.

"Well, it'll give me peace of mind. Come on, I slipped in some of the caramel ice cream you love," he says, while standing from his chair.

At the mention of caramel ice cream, I'm up and out of my seat so fast before following Mikhail through to the kitchen.

Chapter Thirteen

Weddings are supposed to be a celebration. Of love, commitment— all that shit. And they are. This one was all the above, but it's also the worst kind of trigger for Santo. He hid it from Gio well. His distress. The fact that he's mourning his dead fiancée while our big brother is marrying someone he's only just met.

I've been watching him all night. My heart fucking hurts for the guy. He's not himself, not that I'd expect him to be. But, fuck, seeing your brother, your flesh and blood, completely lose his mind to the point that he's talking to ghosts... it's unnerving.

"Santo, why don't I get you a coffee?" I suggest, while reaching for the bottle of whiskey in his hand.

"I don't need fucking coffee. Leave me alone. I'm talking to Shelli. I need to talk to Shelli," he says, his eyes glued to the blank wall in front of him.

I look to Vin, who's been in here all night with me. We're both at a fucking loss. We've kept this from Gio, not wanting to ruin his big day and all. And I'll continue to keep it from him. Our big brother will take this shit hard, carry the guilt that his wedding has sent Santo backwards in his grief.

"I'm waking Gabe up," I tell Vin while gesturing to Santo. "Don't leave him."

Vin nods his head in acknowledgement and continues to watch Santo have a full-on, one-sided conversation with his dead fiancée.

I turn down the hall and make my way to Gabe's room, my fist hammering on his door as soon as it's within reach. When I don't hear any movement, I bang again. Louder and faster.

"Stop fucking hitting my door, Marcel, unless you want my fist to hit your face," Gabe's voice yells out from the other side. Then the door swings open and I'm met by a glare that would send most men running. "Why the fuck are you banging my door down this early in the fucking morning?"

"Santo's losing it. I've been with him all night. It's your turn." I run a hand over my face. I'm fucking tired.

"What do you mean he's losing it? He was fine when I left last night." Gabe glances over his shoulder, into the room, and I can see what's been keeping him busy—or should I say who? Daisy's dress is laid out by his feet. *Daisy*, as in our new sister-in-law's best friend. Either Gabe doesn't want his balls to stay intact or my brother is just plain stupid. Because messing with one of El's friends is the quickest way to land yourself on her shit list. A list none of us want to be on.

"Well, if you weren't preoccupied, you'd have noticed that he started losing it about an hour after Gio and El went to their room for the night," I grunt.

"Wait here," Gabe says as he's slamming the door

in my face. It only takes a minute before he opens it again.

Pushing off the wall, I follow him down the path that leads to Santo's room. "So Daisy, huh? Thought it was a onetime thing?" I ask him.

"Shut it. You didn't see anything. You don't know anything," Gabe grinds out.

"Oh, it's like that? Fine, I didn't see the exact same dress Daisy was wearing on your floor this morning." I laugh.

"I mean it, Marcello. She doesn't want people to know," he says, his tone taking on a more serious note.

"And you do? El is going to give you hell if she finds out. She was very vocal about us not fucking her friends," I remind him of the stakes of this secret relationship of his.

"It's not like that."

"So, I can assume you'll be the next one exchanging vows." I raise a brow at him.

"Let's not get ahead of ourselves," Gabe groans, before quickly changing the subject. "What's Santo been doing?"

"Besides drinking himself stupid? He's talking to Shelli. It's like he can see her or at the very least it's like he thinks he can. It's fucking creepy." A cold shiver runs down my spine. I just can't shake the eeriness of all this.

"What if he can? I mean, no one knows for sure, right?" Gabe asks.

"Yeah, I'm not buying it. His head is messed up. He needs help, like professional help. Not the sort we can give him." I might believe in curses and shit, but seeing dead people? I don't think so.

Vin stomps the toe of his shoe into the ground as we approach the room. I don't need to see it to know what the kid's been up to. I can smell that shit a mile away. I wait for Gabe to start in on a lecture about the weed. We might sell some shit, but we don't ever indulge.

"Don't let Gio see you doing that," Gabe says, and I swear my head spins around like one of those stupid cartoon characters. Maybe Daisy literally fucked his brains out.

"Good thing he's too busy playing house then." Vin laughs.

We all pile into Santo's room, and I stand back and let Gabe take over. Hoping like fuck he can talk some sense into our brother.

"Santo, you good?" Gabe asks.

Santo turns his head and smiles at Gabe like a kid on fucking Christmas morning. It's scary as fuck.

"Shelli's here. Come and say hello, Gabe. She's back."

Gabe glances over his shoulder at me and Vin. I shrug while giving him one of those *I've got no fucking idea* looks. Then Gabe sits next to Santo and looks at the wall. "Hi Shelli," he says.

"She's come back," Santo repeats.

"Yeah? Did she say why she left?" Gabe asks him.

They aren't facing my way but I can see the way Santo's body stiffens. "No. Why'd you leave, Shelli?" he asks the empty space.

"What'd she say? I didn't hear her," Gabe questions, and I have to give it to him. He's handling this talking to dead people shit a hell of a lot better than I could.

"She said she didn't want to, but it's okay because she's back now."

Gabe looks at me again. I don't know what he's expecting me to do. I've been trying to figure out this shitshow all fucking night. "Oh, good. Maybe you and Shelli should get some rest, mate. We've got a plane to catch in a few hours."

"Yeah, good idea," Santo agrees and lies on the bed while Gabe makes his way over to me. "Make sure Gio knows Shelli's coming home."

Gabe nods before exiting the room with Vin and me close on his tail. "What the fuck was that?" he asks as soon as the door clicks closed.

"That was our brother finally losing any sense of reality he had left," Vin says.

"We need to find a way to help him. We can't let him continue to spiral," I chime in.

"We need to get him to pull back on the drinking. Let's start with that," Gabe suggests. "When we get home, we need to find more shit for him to do. Give him shit to occupy his time."

"Might be a good start." I nod.

"What if it doesn't work? What if he's lost and we can't get him back?" Vin asks.

"We don't give up on each other. Ever. If he can't fight for himself, then we fight for him. We will find a way to get him back," Gabe says.

"You two go. I'll stay and make sure he falls asleep," Vin replies.

As soon as I get back to my room, I take a quick

shower and then message Zoe. She's probably asleep, but I need to talk to her.

ME:

Hey.

The little dots pop up and then her name flashes across the screen. I immediately answer the call before pressing the phone to my ear.

"Why are you up so early?" she asks.

"Why are you?" I counter.

"I had a little body in my bed kicking at me all night," she says.

Yesterday, she mentioned that her family came to town. She's told me a bit about them. I know that Mikhail and Izzy, the people who took Zoe in, have three little kids that she adores. What I don't know is how she came to live with them. That's a question for another time, though.

"Yeah? Should I be jealous someone other than me is in your bed?"

"Probably." She laughs. "Why are you awake, Marcel?"

"I've been up all night with Santo. He, uh, he didn't handle the whole wedding thing all that well."

"What happened?" she asks.

"He started talking to his fiancée as if she'd come

back from the dead," I say. "He was drunk, obviously, but still."

"I'm sorry. That must be hard," she replies without the hint of judgement in her voice. "On you as well as on him."

"Yeah, it's not easy. Tell me something good."

"You're coming home today. You still coming over tonight?" she asks.

"Try to keep me away," I tell her. "Is your family still going to be in town?"

"No, they're leaving around noon."

"Pity, I would have loved to meet them," I admit.

"Yeah, let's not do that yet," she says. "Lucy wants to do a double date this week. But it's okay if that's not your thing. I can tell her no."

"A double date with Lucy and Dom? Why not? Should be fun," I say while thinking a date with Dominic McKinley will be anything but fun.

"Are you sure?" Zoe asks.

"If you're there, I'm there, babe. Let's do it."

"Thank you. I gotta go, but I'll see you tonight."

"See you then." I hang up, fall back on my bed, and close my eyes. I just need a little catnap and then I'll be ready to deal with the flight home.

Chapter Fourteen

"You look nervous," I tell Marcel as we walk into the restaurant.

"Is Mikhail having you tailed?" he asks me.

"Why?"

"Because two Russians have been following us since we left your house."

I look behind me, but I don't see anyone. "He mention he was going to have me watched."

"Well, in that case, let's give 'em something to report back on," Marcel says and then I'm being dipped backwards before his lips are pressing onto mine.

Holy freaking shit. I've seen this move on tv, read about it in books. But the real thing? Apart from the fear that I'm about to go splat against the floor, it's way better than what I ever would have thought. When Marcel pulls me upright again, my head spins from that Hollywood-worthy kiss.

"You okay?" he asks while smirking down at me.

"Uh-huh. That was... unexpected."

"Good. Can't become too predictable on you, now can I?" He winks. Then, with my hand in his, Marcel guides me into the restaurant.

I thought that the whole double-date thing would be fun. But now, I kind of wish I had Marcel to myself. I'm not used to this dating thing, and to be sitting across from a forever couple like Lucy and Dominic has my anxiety climbing.

"You look beautiful," Marcel says.

"Thank you." I glance at the booth where Lucy and Dom are already waiting for us. I've known them for a few years now. I shouldn't be nervous.

But then I start to wonder if it's nerves... or envy.

I used to want what they have, before I accepted the fact that I couldn't be someone's everything. That I'd just be a burden. Marcel and I are having fun. I like being with him. I've enjoyed the dates he's taken me on. I love having him in my bed.

But are we destined for anything more? I don't think so. And that just makes me sad, because I can see myself wanting to be with Marcel for a really long time.

"You know we can leave anytime you want," he says, keeping his voice low.

"Why would we leave?"

"Because you look like you'd rather be anywhere else right now, Zoe."

"I'm just nervous. I don't want to embarrass you in front of your friends," I tell him.

"They're your friends too, remember? And, babe, there is literally nothing you could do that would ever embarrass me. One, I don't give a single fuck about what anyone else thinks. Two, you are fucking perfect just the way you are and anyone who says otherwise can book a meeting with the barrel of my gun."

I can't for the life of me think of a reply to all of

that. So I smile up at him. "Let's do this. I can do this," I say more to myself.

Marcel waits for me to slide into the booth before he sits next to me. Lucy scoots around and wraps her arms around me while Domonic and Marcel exchange brief handshakes.

"Double dating. Pretty sure this is what best mates do." Marcel grins at Dominic.

"Acquaintances also have dinner together, Marcello. Don't overthink it," Dom replies.

"Dominic McKinley, play nice," Lucy scolds.

"Little Bee, I'm always nice."

Marcel snorts and then tries to cover it with a cough. "Nicest bloke I know, Lucy. It's why I picked him to be my best mate."

"When is Izzy coming back to town?" Dom directs to me. "I can't imagine he'll last more than two minutes in a room with her."

I lift a shoulder into a half shrug. "Probably not, but she already likes him."

"I doubt that," Dom grunts.

"She does. I told her how nice he is, and how good he is to me. Mikhail and Izzy are firmly on Team Marcel." They're probably not, but I decide to go with the whole *fake it until you make it* approach.

"What's not to like?" Marcel laughs before turning his glare on Dom and Lucy. "So, you two lovebirds plan an actual date yet? I need notice to get my best man tux pressed."

"You're not best man material, and when we have a date, you'll be the last to know," Dominic tells him.

"I'm confused. I thought you two were friends." I gesture from Dominic to Marcel.

"We are," Marcel says at the same time Dominic says, "We aren't."

"Right, well, glad that's cleared up." I shake my head.

"They're friends. Dominic just has a hard time showing anyone he actually likes them, unless it's me, of course." Lucy grins. Then she picks up the menu from the table. "What are you eating? Want to share a starter?"

I follow her lead and start reviewing my options. One thing I love about living in Australia is the food. I thought I knew good food, and then I came here. Although I'd kill for a slice of authentic New York pie right now too.

"Sure, what are you thinking?" I ask Lucy.

"How about we share the calamari and shrimp

cocktails? And then for mains, I think I want the stuffed chicken breast." Lucy snaps the menu shut before setting it back down on the table.

"Sounds great," I say, then turn to Marcel. "What are you eating?" I can't decide. It all looks so good.

"Steak. What do you feel like?" he asks me.

"All of it." I laugh. "I don't know. Um, I think the fish." I settle for the one item my eyes keep going back to. And just as I'm about to close the menu and set it on the table, my body is being pushed down before something heavy lands on top of me.

"Stay down," Marcel grinds out between clenched teeth.

Then I hear a bunch of popping noises mixed with the sounds of people screaming and glass shattering. Marcel doesn't move, using his body as a shield to cover mine.

"What...?" I start to ask and then stop.

"It's okay. Just stay down," he says, his voice calmer than it should be.

Seriously, how the hell is he so calm right now?

When the popping stops, and we hear the squeal of tyres get farther and farther in the distance, Marcel slowly pushes up to his knees with a gun in his hand—though I have no idea where it came from or when he drew it. He glances around the room before calling out to Dom.

"We're good," Dom replies while shoving the table out of his way. I follow the sound of his voice and gasp. There's a trail of blood dripping down his arm.

"You sure about that, mate?" Marcel juts his chin towards the red seeping through Dom's shirt.

"It's just a scratch." Dom stands, scanning the room before pulling his fiancée to her feet. Lucy looks shaken and hasn't said a word since everything went to shit.

I push up off the ground, and Marcel shoves me behind him again. Which seems unnecessary, considering the shooting has stopped. I don't think whoever it was is still here. "You okay, Lucy?" I ask.

"Huh?" She looks to me, and that's when I realise how pale she is.

"Little Bee? It's okay. I've got you. Come on, let's get out of here." Dominic takes her hand in his and starts guiding her towards the door.

"You need a doctor, Dom," Marcel calls out after him.

"I need to get my fiancée out of here," he counters.

I'm about to suggest we do both, get a doctor *and*

get the hell out of here, when two visibly angry Russians storm inside. "Zoe, we need to go."

I know these two guys, Ivan and Kon. I also know I'm not going anywhere without Marcel. "I'm good," I tell them.

Kon glances from Marcel, back to me again. "We need to get you out."

"I'm taking her home. You two can follow," Marcel chimes in.

Ivan looks Marcel up and down, his face twisted in disgust when he says, "We don't take orders from you."

"Yeah? How about you call that boss of yours and explain to him why you're standing around a fresh crime scene arguing with me instead of letting me get his daughter out of here?" Marcel takes my hand and storms past them. "Get in my car," he tells Dom. "I've got the doc meeting us at Zoe's."

Without argument, Lucy and Dom climb into the back of Marcel's SUV. And I turn to see two very displeased-looking Russians behind me. "I'll meet you guys back at my house," I tell them.

"You should come with us, Zoe," Ivan says.

"I'll be fine. I'm calling Mikhail now." I offer him a tight smile while pulling my phone out of my pocket. As soon as the car door closes, I dial Mikhail's number. I know if I don't let him know what just happened, I'll never hear the end of it. And I'll have more than just two Russian shadows following me around. I'll end up with a whole damn army.

By the time Marcel pulls into my driveway, I've managed to convince Mikhail that I'm okay and don't need him to fly back out here. Or at least I think I have. Truth is, I wouldn't be surprised if he ends up on my doorstep in a day or two.

"I'm sorry." I turn in my seat to look at Lucy and Dom.

"This isn't your fault, Zoe," Dom says.

"Lucy?"

"Yeah, sorry. It's okay. It's just a scratch. The doctor's going to patch you right up, Dominic," she says.

"Yeah, just a scratch, babe. It'll take a lot more than someone's bad aim to take me out." Dominic laughs.

"Like a bee?" Marcel questions.

"Not funny, Marcel," Lucy groans.

"I thought it was." Marcel cuts the engine and we all climb out of the car. There's an older man waiting at my front door. I'm assuming he's the doctor.

I grip on to Marcel's hand as we approach. I'm doing my best to hold my shit together. I was just shot at—well, I was in a restaurant that was just shot at. Who were they even aiming for?

I look to Marcel and notice a few fresh scrapes on his face. "Were they shooting at you?" I ask him.

"I honestly don't know, babe. But I'll find out," he says before extending a hand towards the older man. "Doc, thanks for coming."

I unlock the door and usher everyone into the living room. "I'm going to make tea," I say, excusing myself and walking out. When I get to the kitchen, I'm not surprised to find Mikhail's men already standing there.

"You sure you're okay, Zoe?" Kon asks.

"I'm fine," I tell him. "Did Mikhail call you?"

"He did." He nods.

Guess that's that then. I'm stuck with these two for the foreseeable future. There's no point trying to fight Mikhail on this his protectiveness. Although I'm certain that tonight was simply a case of wrong place, wrong time. It has to be, because the idea that someone out there actively wants to hurt Marcel isn't one I care to entertain. Even if I do understand the likelihood of that happening in his line of work, I'm choosing to stay firmly footed in the land of denial right now.

Chapter Fifteen

She should have been home half an hour ago. I've been sitting in her room, on this uncomfortable-as-fuck chair for two hours, waiting for her. I don't know what's keeping her and it's starting to send me into a spiral.

I pull my phone out of my pocket and check my notifications. Nothing. I've left her two voicemails in the last ten minutes, two messages she hasn't responded to. How many more can I leave before it's considered obsessive? Or stalkerish? Then again, do I even fucking care how I come across?

I inhale a deep breath before typing out a text to Vin. I've had him following her around for the last couple of days. Ever since the shooting at the restaurant, where my best friend caught a fucking bullet in his arm. Of course, Dom claims it was nothing more than a scratch, even after the doc fished around and pulled out the piece of lead. Then he insisted on walking the streets with me, trying to find out whatever we could.

We're still fucking looking. All I have to go on is the make and model of the car the assholes were driving. No one knows shit about who it was, or who they were targeting. I've gone through the security tapes, checked the identities of everyone in that restaurant at the time. And no one else seems to be a viable target. Me? Well, the De Bellis family has a long list of enemies. Especially since our father's out of the picture.

Fuckers take Gio for an idiot. They underestimate him and us. My brothers are ready for this. I'm ready for it. No one is taking our family's position in the Melbourne underground.

ME:

Where is she?

VIN:

Pulling into the drive of her house.
Where are you?

ME:

Thanks. You can go home.

Vin doesn't respond. I know he'll either go home or wherever else it is he goes when no one is watching him. I should probably find out what he's been up to. He's not even eighteen yet. We're all supposed to be keeping an eye on the kid. Then again, it's not like he's ever had parental supervision to begin with. It was always Gio and Santo taking care of us younger siblings. Gio told us about our mother, how she was sweet, how much she loved us.

I don't remember her at all. Truth is, I've never even seen a picture of the woman. Our father had everything removed from the house. So, other than the description Gio gave me, I don't know shit about her.

People say you can't miss what you've never had. That's bullshit, because there was a time when I missed having a mother. Now, I don't care. But back then, I would have given anything to meet her, just once.

The bedroom door opens, and I straighten in the chair. I was so lost in my thoughts the sound got me by surprise. Judging by the hand firmly pressed on Zoe's chest, I'm not the only one caught off-guard.

"Marcel? What the hell are you doing sitting in the dark? And how'd you get in here?" she asks while flicking on the light.

"Close the door," I tell her.

Zoe looks at me, and for a brief second, I think she's going to tell me where to go. She doesn't. Instead, she closes the door and walks towards me. "How'd you get in?" she asks again.

"Surprisingly, it wasn't hard. But don't worry, I have a guy coming tomorrow to fix the holes in your security system," I tell her. "Why didn't you answer my messages?"

"What messages?" Zoe digs through her bag, then quickly curses under her breath. "Shit."

"What?"

"My phone, it's not in here. I swear I picked it up when I left the office." She sets her bag down on the bed and starts rummaging through it before emptying the contents out. After another minute or two, she looks up at me. "I must have left it at the office."

"Want me to send someone to get it for you?"

"No, it's okay. I'll just get it in the morning." She shoves everything back into her bag, glancing in my direction when she's done. "Is there a reason you're creeping around my house in the dark?"

"Besides wanting to see you?" I shrug. "No."

"Well, you're seeing me now. What are you going to do with me?" Zoe places her bag on the floor by the bed and kicks off her heels.

"Right now, I'm going to watch you strip out of those clothes." I gesture a hand up and down her body.

Without a word, Zoe unbuttons the front of her blouse, the silky material sliding off her arms and pooling by her feet. Then I watch as she unzips her skirt before it falls to the floor too. When she reaches for her bra next, I lift a hand to stop her.

"Leave it on." My eyes flick over the fire-red lingerie. Matching lace, with sparkly straps. Yeah, I'm not letting that go to waste. "Come here." I crook my index finger at her as my legs spread open, my cock pressing against the fabric of my pants, trying to break free. Undoing my belt, I pop the button of my pants. Zoe stops when she's right in front of me. "On your knees, babe. I want you on your knees," I tell her.

She drops to her knees with her hands on my

thighs and a smirk on her face. "What else do you want?" she says, her voice husky with need before her tongue darts out to lick her bottom lip.

"Take out my cock," I instruct, groaning when her hands move higher up my thighs. Her fingers slowly undo the zipper on my pants, reach into by briefs, and then her palm wraps around my shaft. "Fuck me, even your hand feels fucking amazing."

"If you think my hand feels good, then this is going to blow your mind." Zoe grins as her mouth closes over the tip of my cock.

"Fuck yes." Scooping her hair out of her face, I watch in awe as she takes me deeper. "So damn beautiful," I groan.

When I hit the back of her throat, it takes all of my control not to come right here and now. Zoe moans as she peers up at me, sending vibrations through my balls, and then she fucking swallows.

"Fuck!" I growl out. I take hold of her face. My hands shake and my thighs tense, the urge to take over and fuck her mouth so fucking strong.

Almost like she knows just what she's doing to me, Zoe smiles around my cock, flattening her tongue before she slides back up to the tip.

I cup her cheeks. "Let me know if you need me to stop. Just tap my leg," I tell her before I take over this show and guide my cock back down her throat. I continue pumping in and out of her, holding her face still, at just the right angle. I'm not going to last long. Her mouth feels too fucking good. "I'm gonna come. Are you going to swallow everything I give you, Zoe?"

Her little nod gives me the permission I was seeking before I let go and release right down her throat. Zoe swallows every single drop I give her. Then, she shocks me by sticking out her tongue and licking the remaining cum from my cock. I pick her up and walk over to the bed, throwing her down in the middle of the mattress before climbing on top and covering her body with mine.

"That was fucking amazing," I tell her. My lips descend onto hers. I push my tongue into her mouth and taste myself on her.

Zoe's legs wrap around my back, locking me against her. Not that she needs to do that. I don't plan on leaving this spot anytime soon. I had a rule. *Always make sure she comes first.* That rule just got broken and now I need to rectify this situation. I'm not leaving this bed until I pull at least five orgasms from her body.

Shifting my weight, I force her legs to fall open before moving my mouth down across her cheek until I reach her ear. My hand cups her pussy. "This. It's mine," I whisper. "I like to take care of things that are mine, Zoe."

"Okay," she moans. "Take care of it then."

"Say it first." I move my fingers through the lips of her pussy, on top of the lace that still covers her.

"Say what?" she asks, her hands clinging around my neck.

"That it's mine. That I own this. That you belong to me." I nibble on her ear, only to realise I've said the wrong thing a second after I say it.

Zoe's whole body stills beneath me, her nails dig into the skin on my shoulders, and she shoves at my chest.

I jump off the bed and stare down at her. She has tears running down her face as she scrambles up the bed before pressing her back against the headboard. "I don't belong to anyone. I'm my own person. I'm not..." She's looking right at me but I don't think she's seeing me at all.

Chapter Sixteen

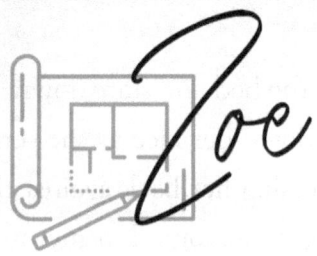

I belong to myself. Not to him. *Not to anyone.*
Nobody will ever own me again. I won't let
them. I can't go back to that. He doesn't
own me.

Please, God, tell me he isn't like those
other men...

Looking up at Marcel, I can see the questions in

his eyes. They've been there for a while but he's never asked, and I've been thankful for that. I wasn't ready to tell him about my past. Honestly, I'm not sure I'm ready to tell him now either. Except some part of me feels like I either have to tell him or ask him to leave and never come back.

It's not fair for me to put him in this position. He's standing at the end of the bed, staring back at me. I know he's waiting... for something. I just don't know what it is.

I close my eyes and let out a sigh. When I open them again, he's still looking at me. "I'm sorry."

"What did I do? What did I say that triggered you?" he asks.

I shake my head. *I can't tell him.* He's not going to want anything to do with me if I do. If I tell him the truth. After I told Flynn, everything changed. He couldn't handle it. Who could?

Marcel slowly moves onto the bed, crawling over the mattress until he's right in front of me. My knees are drawn up, my arms wrapped around them. Taking my hands in his, he squeezes once, forcing me to meet his eyes.

"Whatever it is, I need to know so I don't do it again," he says. "I never want to do something that you don't want."

"I'm sorry," I repeat.

"I'm gonna hedge a guess it was the ownership thing?" He lifts a questioning brow.

I nod and stare at our joined palms again. Marcel pulls his hand free and uses it to tilt my chin upwards until my eyes meet his. "They were just words, Zoe. I don't physically own you. You can't own a human."

"You can actually," I admit.

"What do you mean?"

I don't know what I'm doing, why I feel like I just need to tell him my story. Maybe it'll make him leave me, and then I won't have to worry about trying to be good enough for him.

"I was owned. When I was seventeen, my father owed some people—*some very bad people*—a lot of money. He didn't have it, so he gave me to them instead. As payment. The men then auctioned me off to recoup their losses, I guess. And I was... Well, someone bought me. I was owned... and he..." My heart races. My eyes burn. I can't keep going. I shake my head and skip to the end. "Mikhail and Izzy found me. They saved me."

"Zoe, I'm sorry that happened to you. I really fucking am. No one should ever go through something like that. If those fuckers were still alive, I'd end them. But something tells me Mikhail and Izzy got to them first," Marcel says, his voice calm. So eerily calm.

I nod. "They're all dead. They can't find me anymore. But I can't go back to that. I don't want to be owned. By anyone. Ever."

"That's never going to happen to you again, Zoe. I won't let it." Marcel picks me up, settling me on his lap before his lips press to my forehead. "I promise I won't ever let anything happen to you."

"You can't promise that. You can't control the world," I tell him, and he grins.

"Watch me."

I climb off his lap and off the bed, walking into my bathroom. Where I grab the robe from the back of the door, shoving my arms through the sleeves and wrapping the soft fabric around myself. "It's okay if you want to leave. You don't have to stay," I say as soon as I walk back out to the bedroom.

"You want Chinese or pizza?" he asks, ignoring the easy out I just gave him.

"What?"

"For dinner, Chinese or pizza?"

"Pizza?" I reply, though I can hear the question in my voice. I'm still confused as to what is going on right now, why Marcel isn't running for the hills.

"Great. Pick a movie. I'll order the food." He taps the empty side of the bed, his way of telling me to join him.

I really don't know how I found this guy, or why he's being so understanding of my issues. I get I probably can't keep him, but I'd sure like to.

"Oh, by the way, we're having dinner at my house tomorrow night, with my brother and El. She's, ah, been through a lot lately and I figured a family dinner will do them good. And truth is, it's probably about time you met them," Marcel says casually.

I stare at him, open-mouthed. "You want me to meet your family?"

"Yes." That's all he gives me. No further explanation.

"What if... I don't know, Marcel. I can't control when I'm going to freak out."

"First of all, you don't freak out, babe. It's your body's reaction to a past traumatic event. Completely normal. Second, I couldn't give a fuck if you did. I'll be there, and if you need to leave, I'll get you out of there so fast your head will spin. Now, pick a movie, and don't overthink it. It's just dinner."

Just dinner. It's not just dinner, though. It's meeting the family.

I'm nervous, but that's to be expected, right? Meeting the family for the first time isn't the easiest thing I've ever had to do. It's not the hardest either. But I want Marcel's family to like me. I never had a huge family growing up. It was always just my mother, my father, and me. They didn't have a bunch of relatives—well, none that I knew of.

Now, I have Mikhail and Izzy. The whole Valentino/Petrov clan. Although they didn't have much choice when it came to accepting me or not. I think they're all afraid of what Izzy would do to them if they didn't.

A man who looks just like Marcel, except crankier, walks in first. Followed by another man and then a woman. I'm gathering the last to enter are Gio and Eloise. Marcel's eldest brother has that presence around him that screams *boss*. I've met enough of them now to know it. It's the woman who has my skin going cold, though.

"Everyone, this is Zoe. Zoe, this is everyone," Marcel says.

"Hi, I'm El. It's so great to meet you," the woman says with a small, tight smile. Forced or pained. From the looks of her, maybe a bit of both.

I can't stop staring at her. Someone's hurt her. How is she standing here pretending she's okay with her face covered in bruises?

"Hi. Zoe. Can you... ah... show me to the bathroom?" I introduce myself while my thoughts are going a million miles an hour, trying to figure out a way to get her away from the men in this room.

Eloise looks to her husband and I can see the terror in her eyes.

"I can show you," Marcel says.

"No, it's fine. I can take her." Eloise pushes up from her chair and starts to manoeuvre around Gio.

"You don't have to do that, Ellie," he whispers but I hear him.

"I want to," she responds, and I follow her out of the dining room, glancing over my shoulder. Watching everyone *watch* us leave.

As soon as we turn the corner, I step up next to her, being sure to keep my voice low. "I can get you out of here."

"Excuse me?" She stops short.

"I can get you out. You don't have to stay here," I tell her.

Eloise moves back a step, putting distance between us almost like she's afraid I might hurt her. "What are you talking about?"

"It's okay. I can help. Who did that to your face? Was it your husband? I can help you." Truth is, I *need* to help her. I can't just leave her here.

"You think my husband did this? To me?" She shakes her head. "He didn't. He wouldn't, and if you knew any of those men in there, you'd also know that none of them are capable of hurting a woman." Then her arm shoots out, gesturing behind me. "The bathroom is down the hall, third door on the left." Before I can respond, she's already walking away. Back towards the dining room.

I can't stay here. I need to get out of this house. I tried to do the right thing, offer her help. What can I do if she doesn't want it? I don't know, but I'm not sticking around to find myself trapped in another nightmare. So I do the only thing I can.

I run. Or at least I attempt to.

"Zoe?" Marcel's voice follows me down the hall, and then he's in front of me. "Are you okay?"

There's so much concern on his face when he looks at me like this. It's hard to believe that he would sit by and let a woman be abused. But I also saw *her* face, and I can't unsee that. "I... ah... I forgot I had a thing to do. At home."

"Don't leave. Whatever happened... I'm sure we can work it out," he says.

"I can't." I shake my head and take a step back.

"Follow me." Marcel grabs my hand. His grip isn't tight though. He keeps it loose, giving me the ability to pull back if I want to.

It's the little things he does that make me feel safe with him. Things like this. I just don't know if I'm being an idiot or not. My feet follow him up the stairs and then I find myself standing in a bedroom. His bedroom.

Chapter Seventeen

S he's ready to flee. I can see it in her eyes. She's scared and I fucking hate seeing her like this. I don't think she's afraid of me, though. It's something else. I have no idea what happened with her and El.

All I know is that El came back into the dining room shaking. But being away from Gio does that to her lately, even if he's just out of reach. I didn't tell Zoe about Ellie's attack. I mean, how do you bring up that your sister-in-law was raped and beaten? It doesn't exactly come up in conversation. Especially when I knew that Zoe was already struggling with her own inner demons.

In hindsight, I probably should have told her, prepared her for what she'd see.

Truth is, I selfishly thought I wouldn't *have* to tell her. Zoe finding out that we have no fucking way of keeping our women safe is the last thing I want. She was already on the fence, and now she's going to know there's no escaping the De Bellis curse.

"Tell me what you're thinking. Because I'm pretty sure, whatever it is, it's way off from the actual truth." Walking into my closet, I open a drawer and pull out the red-ribboned bracelet I was given as a child. It was a gift from an old Italian woman, one of the wives of a soldier.

She was the one who told me about the curse and then handed me the red ribbon, claiming it would protect me. I was ten back then. A kid who rushed back home and hid his latest trinket before his father could throw it away. After Shelli, I dug the thing out of an old shoe box. Even wore it for a couple of days before I felt like a fucking idiot believing a ribbon could protect us from anything.

The old woman was wrong, though. Because it's not me who needs protecting. It's not my brothers either. It's the women we bring into the family. It's Zoe.

I walk back out of the closet, clutching the red ribbon in my fist. "This is going to sound crazy and it is. But I'm going with it anyway, because if there's the tiniest hint of truth to it, I'd rather you be protected as much as you can be."

"What are you talking about?" Zoe asks.

I open my hand and watch her eyes flick down to my palm before looking up at me again. "Remember how I told you that my family's cursed?" She nods, and I continue. "Well, it's something I've known for a long time. It's why Shelli is dead, why El looks the way she does right now. And it's why I should let you walk away. I don't want to lose you, though, Zoe. So I'm going to need you to wear this instead."

Her eyebrows draw down in confusion. "What do you mean? Who did that to El's face?"

"A family looking to hurt Gio, and they used his wife to do it."

"I... I'm sorry."

"Will you wear this?" I lift the ribbon between my fingers and hold it out to her again.

"It's a piece of ribbon, Marcel," she says like I don't already know that. I told her it was crazy. But right now, I don't care.

"Someone gave that to me when I was young. Told me it would protect me against the curse. But today I realised something. I don't need protection, Zoe. But you do. So please humour me and wear it."

She holds out her right arm and I slide the ribbon over her hand before tightening it around her wrist.

"Thank you," I tell her.

"I'm not saying I believe you're cursed, but if it makes you feel better, I'll wear it." Zoe walks over to my bed and sits herself on the edge of the mattress. "What happened to El?"

I still. How the fuck do I answer that? I don't want to tell her too much. Not because I don't trust her, but because I don't want her to feel unsafe with me. Arming her with the knowledge that I can't do shit to protect her against the kind of thing that happened to my sister-in-law is only going to send her running again.

I wouldn't blame her either. After what she's already experienced in her life, she'd be mad to stay. That doesn't mean I want her to go, though.

"Marcel? What happened?" Zoe asks again.

"She was showing a property to a client when he attacked her. She was alone and... You know what? Let's talk about something else. Like how fucking hot you look in that dress and how much better it's going to look once it's on my floor." I close the distance before dropping to my knees in front of the bed. In front of Zoe. With my hands on her thighs, I slowly pry them apart, giving her plenty of opportunity to stop me if she wants to. "Fuck, this is the prettiest thing I've ever seen," I grunt when I'm greeted by the sight of her lace-covered pussy.

"Do you think we should talk?" Zoe suggests.

My eyes shift from her pussy to her face, while one side of my mouth tilts upwards. "You want to talk, babe? Want to hear about how hard my cock is right now? How I can smell your arousal?" My hand slides higher up her thigh. "Want to talk about how I'm going to make you come? First on my fingers." Pushing the lace aside, I glide two digits through her wet lips before sliding them inside her. "Once my hand is coated in your juices, I'm going to make you come all over my tongue. And then, just when you think you can't possibly take anymore, you're going to come all over my fucking cock."

I pump my fingers in and out of her. She's so

fucking wet, so close to falling over the edge already. Zoe's body drops backwards onto the bed.

"You want that, babe? You want me to make you come, over and over again?" I continue to pump my fingers in and out. The walls of her pussy convulse, sucking me in. "Or I could stop and we can talk about something else?" My hand stills as I quirk a brow.

"Don't you dare fucking stop, Marcello." Zoe pushes up on her elbows to glare at me.

I smile and start moving again. "Wouldn't dream of it. Now, are you going to be a good girl and drench my hand?" I pump harder, curling my fingers upwards. Rubbing against that magic little spot inside her. Then, pressing my thumb against her clit, I draw circles as I pump two fingers in and out of her pussy.

"Oh god! Marcel, don't stop." Zoe moans. Her thighs shake and her hips gyrate in rhythm with my movements. "Shit!" she screams right before her entire body locks up. And then she's coming.

"That's it, fucking beautiful." I pull my hand back before she has time to recover.

I hold her pussy open and slide my tongue through the centre. From bottom to top. I don't know what this girl eats, but whatever it is, I need to buy it in bulk. Because, fuck, she tastes good. So fucking good. I circle my tongue around her clit, applying more pressure with each stroke. My fingers dig into the soft flesh of her upper thighs as I continue to spread them wide. My mouth closes around her clit and I suck while flicking my tongue over her sensitive bud. Zoe's hands grip my head, pushing my face into her pussy. Not that I could physically get any closer if I tried.

Trust me, nothing's ripping my mouth away from this piece of heaven.

It doesn't take long before Zoe's coming apart on my tongue, her fingers pulling at the strands of my hair. Straightening up, I stare down at her. She looks spent, but I've still got one more orgasm I want to wring from her.

"Ready for the trifecta, babe?" I flip her over onto her stomach. I position her so she's on her knees, lift her dress over her ass, and slide her panties down her thighs. Then I dig into my back pocket and pull out a condom. "I need words, Zoe. Do you want me to make you come on my cock?" I ask. Flicking my button open, sliding my zip down, and freeing my cock.

"Yes, I want that. Please," she says, looking back over her shoulder at me.

I step up behind her, freeing my cock and sheathing it before wrapping her hair around my hand and tugging her head towards me. Leaning forward, I close my mouth over hers as I slide into her slowly. Her pussy tightens around me.

"Mmm... Oh god!" Zoe moans into my lips.

"I love making you come," I grunt, as I straighten up and drive into her. Picking up my pace. Hitting harder and harder with each thrust. "Your cunt was fucking made for me. So fucking tight and wet. Look how she wraps around my cock like a damn glove."

Zoe's walls flex and her juices flood my cock as my words echo through the room. Reaching a hand between us, I rub circles around her clit. I need her to come. I'm not going to last much longer. She feels too fucking good. The tightening of my balls tells me I'm close to losing my load as tingles run up my spine.

"You need to come for me now, Zoe. Fuck!" I growl. "I want it. I fucking need it."

Like the perfect fucking creature she is, her body responds to my commands. Her pussy clings to my cock like it's a fucking lifeline, milking me of everything I have.

A Sinner's Virtue

.   .   .

Chapter Eighteen

I allow myself one last look at Marcel's sleeping body. I don't want to leave. *I have to.* This relationship isn't good for me. He has this control on me, the sort of control that I can't allow to happen. I promised myself I wouldn't waste the second chance at life I was gifted.

If I stay here, I'm going to end up completely under his spell. I let him seduce me last night. I allowed myself to believe in the fairy tale that everything would be fine. It's not going to be. I saw his sister-in-law's face. I don't know everything that happened to her, and maybe my assumptions were wrong. But I do know that I don't want that kind of life. I don't want to be afraid to turn corners. I don't want to look over my shoulder all the time, waiting for something to happen. For Marcel's enemies to come for me.

I like to pretend that I'm strong. I like to portray that I can handle myself. The truth is I can't. I'm just as weak as I was back when my father traded me off at seventeen. The only difference is I hide it better now.

I close the door as quietly as I can, then tiptoe my way down the stairs, hoping like hell that I can make it out of this place unseen. Sighing in relief when I make it to the front door, I pull it open and step outside. However, that relief is short-lived.

A young kid is standing a few feet away while a waft of smoke billows around him. He raises one brow at me. "Sneaking out?"

"I'd say leaving quietly." I smile, hoping I can

just keep walking and not have him question me anymore.

"Marcel know you're *leaving quietly*?" the kid asks while mimicking a bad American accent.

"Mhmm, I'd really love to stay and chat, but I'm kinda in a hurry," I tell him. "It was nice to meet you, though."

"You need a ride, Zoe?"

"No, I have a car coming for me. But thanks anyway." I continue on down the driveway, not daring to look back.

"It's Vin, by the way," he calls out after me.

"What is?" I ask, while glancing over a shoulder.

"My name. You would have been curious if you left without knowing it." He shrugs.

"I would have been. Nice to meet you, Vin." I turn around and walk faster until I reach the gates *and* the two guys currently standing guard there. For a moment, I wonder if they're actually going to let me out of here, and then one of them simply nods his head at me and presses a button that has the metal doors swinging open.

It takes all of my restraint not to run. To remain calm and walk down the street. I don't want to draw any attention to myself. When I turn a corner, I pull out my phone and send a message to Lucy.

ME:

Think you can come and get me?

LUCY:
I KNOW I CAN. WHERE ARE YOU?

I send her the street name and she tells me she'll be here in five. I lean against a tree and wait for her. And true to her word, barely five minutes later, Lucy pulls up in Dominic's Rolls Royce.

Way to be incognito.

"Did you steal your fiancé's car?" I ask her as I jump into the passenger seat.

"He's lucky I don't take a baseball bat to it again." She sighs and I laugh.

"What he do?"

"You don't want to know. Any reason you're sneaking out of the De Bellis mansion at this hour of the morning?"

"Not sneaking out, *leaving quietly*. And, yes. I need to go home for a little bit. I'm really sorry, and I know I'm putting you in the lurch but I need to go to New York. Just for a week, maybe two." My words come out fast and rushed.

"Okay, take as long as you need. We will be fine." Lucy pulls away from the curb. "Where am I taking you?" she asks.

"My place. I need to get my passport and pack a bag."

"If something's wrong, if you're in trouble, you can tell me."

"No, not in trouble. I just need to get away. Clear my head. Think about things, because everything with Marcel is... intense," I tell her.

"Okay, but I'm getting Dom to go grab your passport. If we stop by your place, I guarantee Marcel will be there looking for you before you even step through the front door. So, if you're trying to escape without him catching up, we need to move quickly."

Lucy dials Dom's number and puts the call on speaker. "Little Bee, did you take my car?"

"I did, but it's still in one piece... for now. I need you to go to Zoe's and pick up her passport," Lucy says before turning to me. "Where is it?"

"Top drawer in the office," I tell her.

"You okay, Zoe?" Dom asks through the speaker.

"I'm good. I just need to go back to New York for a week," I reply.

"Dom, get the passport and meet us at the airport. And if Marcel asks, you don't know where Zoe is."

"Sure. Meet you at the airport," Dom says before disconnecting the call.

Walking through arrivals in JFK, I turn my phone back on and then quickly silence it when the notifications start rolling in. I have twenty missed calls from Marcel. I'll call him back soon. I sent him a message as I was boarding, explaining that I was going home for a bit.

I felt guilty for just walking out on him. He hasn't done anything wrong. This is totally a case of *it's not him; it's me*. I don't have the energy to talk to him right now, though. I have a few missed calls and messages from Izzy and then two from Mikhail as well.

As I'm about to call Izzy back, I hear my name being yelled out. Looking up, I find my adoptive mother waving at me as she pushes her way through the crowd very unapologetically.

"Zoe Petrov, get your ass over here," Izzy shouts as she barrels right into me. Her arms wrap around me so damn tight it's hard to breathe. I don't move, though. I need this. I need her. Probably more than I thought I did. My eyes burn with unshed tears. And when Izzy pulls back, she looks me up and down. "I'm going to kill him. What'd he do?"

I shake my head and force a smile. "He didn't do anything. I just missed you guys."

"Bullshit. You haven't been back here since you left, so what did he do?"

"Honestly, nothing. I just... I got scared. It was supposed to be fun, a one-night thing, and now its... Well, it's just a lot."

"You love him?" Izzy asks.

I shrug. "I don't know. I just needed a breather."

"Well, take as long of a breather as you want. Because I, for one, am glad to have you home. You have no idea how much I need some adult conversation in my life," she says. "I spend all day talking to toddlers and babies."

"You have Mikhail," I remind her.

"Like I said, I need *adult* conversation," Izzy deadpans, and I can't hold back my laugh. She has a way of making me feel like everything is going to be okay. I remember when she first found me, and I clung to her like the lifeline she was.

"I'm really sorry I sprung this on you guys and didn't give you notice," I tell her.

"Nonsense. This is your home, Zoe. You don't

need to give anyone notice to come home. Now, come on, let's get out of here before Mikhail sends in the Bratva search team." Izzy links her arm with mine and leads me towards the exit.

"There's a Bratva search team?"

Izzy lifts one shoulder. "No idea, but if there is, they'd never be able to find me if I wanted to stay hidden." She smirks.

"I have no doubt."

"So, lover boy? Does he know you're here?"

"I sent him a message, and I'll call him later. How are the kids?" I ask, changing the topic.

Izzy is a great mother. She can talk about her kids for hours and never run out of things to brag about. As she starts telling me everything the three Valentino-Petrov heirs have been up, I look around the busy airport and it hits me. I'm back in New York. There's a reason I haven't been back here. I've never felt safe outside of the Petrov compound. Thankfully, Izzy doesn't stop talking when I step closer to her, or when my hand clings to her arm just a bit tighter.

I focus on her voice and on breathing as we walk out to where there's a blacked-out SUV waiting for us. One of the Petrov soldiers holds the back door open. And as soon as I'm in the car, I take in a lungful of air. I didn't even realise I was holding my breath.

I can do this. I'm just going to be hanging out at the house. I don't need to go anywhere. And it's only a week. Two tops.

Chapter Nineteen

Three weeks later

Y ou know that whole saying about letting people go and if they come back, they're yours? If they don't, then they never were? Yeah, I call bullshit on that. I've let Zoe go, but every fibre of my being still says that girl is mine.

Of course I can't say shit like that to her, *especially* if I want to get her back. Which I do. I've been patient. At this point, I should be nominated for fucking sainthood on account of that patience.

I don't text and call her nonstop. Well, not after the first week.

Because after that first week, I got the message loud and fucking clear that she wanted space. I know she's scared. I understand why, and most of the time, I actually think she's probably better off as far away from me as she can possibly get. Knowing that doesn't mean I have to fucking like it, though.

I miss her more than I've ever missed anyone before. I'm about ready to give up on the whole Mister Cool-Calm-and-Patient act and get on a flight over to New York. How can she realise that whatever we have is worth fighting for if it's not right in front of her face? If I'm not there to convince her?

This is the very definition of being stuck between a rock and a hard place. Whatever I decide to do, it's the wrong fucking thing. If I stay and wait her out, sit here twisting my thumbs, hoping she'll come back... I might never see her. If I go over there, make a scene, pressure her to come home with me... I might push her away for good.

"You need to get laid," Vin says, walking into the room.

"What I don't need is sex advice from a fucking teenager who doesn't know his dick from his balls," I grunt without bothering to look at him.

"Whatever. I'm not the one with a bad case of blue balls. My balls are getting plenty of love on a daily basis." The asshole laughs.

"Anyone have the safe sex talk with you yet? You better be making sure you're wrapping it before using it. The last thing we need is De Bellis spawn running around." I raise a questioning brow at him.

"Yeah, that's not happening. At least not from me," he replies.

"What are you doing home? Shouldn't you be at school or something?" I ask as soon as I realise it's the middle of the day on a Friday.

"I was at school. I need your car."

I blink at him. The fucker has his own car. In fact, we have multiple cars in the garage. What the fuck does he want with mine?

"Why?"

"Because I need to follow someone, and your car doesn't draw attention." He shrugs.

"Who you following?"

"No one you know. Can I use it or not?"

I consider questioning him more. I *should* question him more, but sometimes it's better not to know what my brothers are up to. "Fine, but don't fuck it up." I pull my keys out of my pocket and toss them his way.

"Thanks, bro. Catch ya 'round," he says before strolling out of the room. Like he doesn't have a care in the world.

"Marcel, wake the fuck up." Santo's voice breaks through my sleep.

"What the fuck? Go and find someone else to piss off," I grunt.

"Get up. Gabe got pinched." My brother's words have my eyes snapping open.

"What the fuck for?" I'm up and off the sofa I fell asleep on God only knows how long ago. One of my brothers getting pinched? It could be for fucking anything.

"They're in Sydney. I don't know everything. Gio just called," Santo says.

"Fuck." I tug my phone out of my pocket and dial Gio's number.

"Marcel, I'm busy. Can it wait?" he answers.

"What'd Gabe get done for?"

"An arms deal," Gio says. "Xavier's on his way up here. We'll get it sorted, but I need you to keep shit under control at home."

"Arms dealing? Fucking hell," I curse under my breath. My brother could be away for a long-ass fucking time for that. "How likely is it that Xavier will get him off?"

Xavier Christianson is the solicitor we keep on retainer. He's also Dom's future brother-in-law.

"No idea, but we'll do everything we can," Gio says before disconnecting the call.

"Okay, we have to keep this shit between us. The last thing we need is the city finding out," I tell Santo.

"Agreed. Where's Vin?"

"No fucking idea, but wherever he is, he has my car," I say. Just as I'm about to reach out to the baby brother in question, Zoe's name flashes across the screen. "Give me a minute." I walk out of the living room and swipe answer. "Hey."

"Marcel, are you busy?" she asks.

"For you? Never. What's wrong?" I'm not sure

what else could possibly fucking happen at this point.

"I, um, I just wanted to hear your voice," she says.

Something isn't right. I've talked to Zoe a few times since she's been gone, but she's never sounded so withdrawn. "What did you do today?"

"I went to a bar. I thought... well, I thought I could do it. You know, it's just a bar. New York is just a city. I should be able to go out to a bar."

"What happened?"

"I'm fucked up is what happened. I couldn't even go to a bar. I feel like I'm never going to be normal again. When I was in Melbourne, I could go out. Now that I'm back here, it's like every step forward I've taken has vanished and I'm back where I started. It's stupid."

"It's not stupid. And there is nothing wrong with how you're feeling. You are strong, Zoe, one of the strongest people I know. You can do anything you want, but you don't have anything to prove to anyone. If you don't feel comfortable going out, then don't go out. If you don't want to be in New York, then come home."

"This is supposed to be my home," she mumbles.

"Where is your heart, Zoe? Wherever your heart wants to be, that's where home is."

"What if my heart doesn't work properly? I don't think I'm strong enough, Marcel. I see the women who survive in this life. They're brave. They fight for what they want. Me? I'm not that brave. I got too close to you and ran."

"That heart of yours is pure, Zoe. Maybe you have enough good in you to outweigh the bad in me? And you don't need to be anyone else. I don't want someone else, babe. I want you, just the way you are," I tell her. I know I'm not good for her, but she's fucking mine anyway.

"What have you been up to? How's school?" she asks, changing the subject.

"School is boring. It was way more fun when you were able to stop in and visit me." I smirk at the memory.

"I bet it was," Zoe says with a little more lightness to her tone.

When Santo steps out of the living room into the hallway with a questioning brow lifted on his face, I know I need to get off the phone and deal with family shit. Honestly, I'd rather be with Zoe. Not that I'm ever going to leave my brother rotting in a damn cell without doing everything I can to help him, though.

Truth is I don't usually get too involved in the family business. Have I done shit that'd give even the demons in hell nightmares? Absolutely. Would I do all of it again? Without a doubt. There is nothing I wouldn't do for my family. No line I wouldn't cross if it meant saving one of my brothers.

"Babe, can I call you back? Santo needs help with something." I can't tell Zoe exactly what it is that Santo needs help with; although I'm sure it won't be long before she hears that one of my brothers is presently behind bars.

"Sure. I'm sorry to bother you."

"You aren't bothering me. I'll call you back," I tell her before hanging up.

"*Babe?* You still holding out hope she's coming back?" Santo says.

"She *is* coming back."

"For how long? You said it yourself. We're fucking cursed, Marcel. There is no happily ever after for any of us," Santo grunts while bringing that ever-present bottle of whiskey to his lips.

I walk over and snatch the bottle from his hand. "This shit ain't going to fucking help right now. Our brother is sitting in a fucking cell. We've got more important shit to do."

"Marcel? What happened?"

I pivot on the heel of my shoe and my heart fucking sinks at the look on Daisy's face. Gabe's girl-friend. Those two have become really serious lately —more so since they're not hiding their relationship anymore. It's the fucking curse. Gabe found his happiness, and now this shit happens.

"It's going to be okay. Gio and Xavier will have him home before you know it, sweetheart," I tell her. I have no fucking idea if that's true or not. But if a little white lie helps wipe that heartbroken look off her face, then that's what I'll do.

"What was he arrested for? Why isn't anyone telling me?" she asks.

I look to Santo. He's no fucking help. The asshole is sprawled out on the sofa with another bottle of whiskey in his hand.

"I'm not sure. We need to wait for Gio and Xavier to fill us in. In the meantime, we need to stay positive. You know, put those good vibes out into the universe. All that juju shit." I'm pulling crap out of my ass now.

"Hey." Vin walks in, looks at Daisy and then over to me. "What's going on?"

"Gabe got pinched in Sydney," I tell him.

"What for?"

"Where's El? Go and see what she wants for dinner," I reply instead of answering his question. I won't lie to my brother, but I also won't tell him in front of Daisy. The last thing this girl needs is to be Googling just how long someone can be put behind bars for fucking arms dealing.

Thankfully, Vin reads the fucking room. Unlike Santo, who's still busy drowning himself in that fucking bottle.

"Come on, Daisy. Let's go find that sister-in-law of mine. Getting her to decide on dinner is like pulling fucking teeth."

"She's not that bad," Daisy says.

"Yes, she is. This one time, we argued for two hours over pizza or fish and chips. Two hours, Daisy. And you know what we ended up with?"

"What?" she asks.

"Both." Vin shakes his head before walking right back out of the room again. "Come on, I'm not dealing with this one alone."

Daisy looks at me and then follows Vin out. She's not stupid. She knows we're trying to distract her, keep her from spiralling over the fact her boyfriend is currently sporting a pair of silver bracelets.

A few hours ago, I was debating on whether or not I was going to get on a flight to New York. Now, I need to go and find out what I'm supposed to be handling while Gio's stuck in Sydney and Santo is out of his fucking mind.

Gabe was the one picking up the slack. He stepped up when Santo needed the break. If Gabe's locked up, that responsibility is going to fall on my fucking shoulders. That's not a job I want. It's one I'll do, if I have to do it. But at the same time, I'll be looking for a way to get Santo back to his old self sooner rather than later. I don't want to be anyone's fucking underboss.

Chapter Twenty

"Are you sure about this?" Izzy asks for the tenth time in the last ten minutes.

"I'm sure. I need to go back, Iz. I can't keep hiding out in this house," I tell her.

"I don't see a problem with you staying and hiding out here forever," Mikhail says, his arms folded across his chest and his signature scowl on his face.

"I know you don't, but it *is* a problem. And as much as I'd love to stay here, it's not what's best for me. I have a good life in Melbourne."

"What if I get rid of him? Your life would be better without him." Mikhail smirks—his way of trying to play off his very real suggestion to get rid of Marcel.

"Don't do that. He's not my problem." I sigh. "I like him. Which is *my problem*. I don't want to like someone this much."

"You deserve to be happy, Zoe," Izzy says while baby Lex babbles at me from where he's perched on her hip.

"I know." I made a decision to go back to Melbourne and to give this thing with Marcel a real chance. I want to be able to have the life that I see others have. I want it so desperately. I just fear I'm never going to be able to.

"This will always be your home, Zoe. You can come back anytime," Mikhail reminds me. "I'll wait out front. I'm driving you to the airport."

"You don't have to do that."

"I know. I want to," he says before walking out of the room. Leaving me alone with Izzy.

"I know that you're an adult, but you're still my responsibility. If you need anything—and I mean anything—you call me." Izzy wraps her free arm around my shoulders and tugs me against her.

"I will. Promise."

The moment I step foot onto the tarmac, I find Lucy waiting for me. Mikhail insisted that I make use of the Petrov jet to get back home. I tried to argue that flying commercial was completely fine, but he wasn't budging. And I didn't have the energy to win the argument this time. Truth is, I'm kind of glad. Flying private is better. Plus, there are no crowds to fight my way through.

Lucy lets out a high-pitched squeal as she runs towards me. Her body slams into mine, and her arms wrap around my neck tight. Too tight.

"Lucy, I can't breathe."

"Oh, shit. Sorry. I'm just so excited you're back. Don't leave me for that long again ever." She pouts while loosening her hold on me slightly.

"Okay," I say. "I missed you too."

"Come on, let's get you home." She releases my body, her arm hooks through mine, and we make our way over to her car.

There's this sense of freedom that comes with being back in Australia. I'm not sure if it's Melbourne in general, or just being away from New York. I tried really hard to fight the panic attacks while I was there. And for the most part, within the walls of the Petrov compound, I was fine. But the few times I tried to venture out... well, that was a different story. Izzy had to talk me down more than once.

It's embarrassing. I should be able to move on. The people who hurt me aren't even alive anymore. Logically, I know they can't come back for me. But there's something about New York that just draws the fear out of me.

I climb into the passenger seat and buckle up because I value my life. And Lucy's driving is... well, let's just say I've seen calmer NASCAR races. "I really am sorry I left you the way I did. At work, I mean. I promise I won't do it again."

"Don't be. It's okay. We all need to get away at times." She lifts one shoulder into a shrug, as if me leaving at the drop of the hat is no big deal.

"So, what'd I miss?" I ask her.

"Apart from one of the De Bellis brothers getting arrested last week? Not a lot."

My heart literally stops in my chest and suddenly I understand the meaning of the phrase *my heart skipped a beat*. I've been talking to Marcel. He's very much not in jail. I try to keep my voice calm as I pivot in my seat to face Lucy. "Who got arrested?"

She turns her head to look at me. "Marcel didn't tell you?"

"No. He didn't."

Why wouldn't he tell me? Maybe I've built this whole relationship up in my head. I could be in this alone. But the way Marcel talks to me... the things he says... They make me feel like he's just as deep in this as I am.

Could I be hearing what I want to hear? Possibly.

"Gabe got arrested in Sydney. I don't know all the details. But I do know that they have my brother as their attorney, so he'll likely get off. Xavier is the best at what he does," Lucy says confidently.

Lucy's brother happens to be Melbourne's best criminal defence attorney. Of course, I've never needed his services, but I have met the guy a few times. And if I ever did need a lawyer, I'd pick him. He's intense and just has that look about him that lets you know there's no point arguing with him because he will win.

"Lover boy really didn't say anything? Odd."

"It's his family, Lucy. And I know how these kinds of things work. He can't tell me. Just like I wouldn't tell him anything I know about Mikhail and Izzy. It's just not how things are done." Even as the words leave my mouth, I can't be sure if I'm trying to convince her or myself. Marcel obviously has reasons for not wanting me to know his brother got arrested. And whatever they are, in the end, the decision to tell me is his to make.

I'm not going to get upset over the fact he doesn't feel like he can confide in me. Why would he? I ran. Whatever we were building scared the crap out of me and I ran to the other side of the world. I've been gone for a month. Yes, we've spoken on the phone every day, exchanged text messages, but that's not the same as being here. Marcel has no reason to trust me, because I haven't given him one.

"If you say so." Lucy shrugs.

As soon as Lucy stops out front of my apartment, I look up and am relieved to see the familiar building. I just want to jump in the shower and then climb into bed. I might have slept on the plane, but I'm still drained. The time difference between the two countries is a lot to get used to. It will take a good three to four days before I'm fully functioning in Aussie time.

"Thank you for picking me up." I lean over the centre console and kiss Lucy on the cheek. "I'll be in the office bright and early tomorrow morning."

"I'll see you then—oh, and say hi to lover boy for me," she replies with a smirk.

I nod, get out of the car, and grab my bag from the trunk. I have no intentions of seeing Marcel yet. I didn't exactly tell him I was coming home today. I don't know why. I just didn't.

I think I want time to settle back into life here before facing him. I also want to see him so much, and like I said to Mikhail, that's a problem. I'm in too deep, and it's only going to get me hurt in the long run.

A few minutes later, I'm walking into my apartment. I drop my bag in the entrance hall and head straight for the bathroom. I need to rinse off the full day's travel and sleep for a decade. Then I'll call Marcel and let him know I'm back.

Chapter Twenty-One

I should wake her up. Let her know I'm here. Instead, I'm watching my girlfriend sleep. Like a fucking creeper. I've been hanging out with Dom too fucking much. Clearly, his stalkerish ways are rubbing off on me.

My girlfriend.

I'm fairly new to the whole girlfriend thing, but I'm pretty sure if you're dating someone and you've been away for a month, you'd tell them you were coming home, right? Well, apparently, *my girlfriend* didn't feel the need to let me know she was home. So here I am, watching her sleep.

I considered climbing into the bed with her. But I didn't want to scare her. That's the only reason my ass is staying firmly planted in this chair. I've been waiting weeks to see her again. It was harder than I thought it would be. I was close to flying over to New York, just to see her. That was before my brother got pinched. And now I'm picking up the fucking pieces, working my ass off to help Gio run the businesses. It's kept me busy, kept my mind preoccupied. So much so that I had to find out from an alert on my phone that someone had entered Zoe's apartment.

I might have put some cameras in here while she was gone, so when the motion detectors went off, the first thing I did was log in. The second thing I did was a double-take when I saw who set them off. If I wasn't knee-deep in some fucker's guts, I would have been here an hour ago. And I mean literally *knee-deep*. Gio had me gut some motherfucker like a fish. He was a manager at one of our strip clubs. The stupid son of a bitch thought we wouldn't notice him stealing from us.

I wonder why she didn't feel the need to tell me she was coming home. I would have picked her up from the airport. I could have given her some *welcome home* orgasms on the way back to her apartment.

My dick hardens at the thought of sinking inside her again. A month of only my hand has been damn near torture. And I know torture. *Trust me.* I don't know how people go so fucking long without sex. I don't plan to ever do it again. Wherever Zoe and her vagina go, I'm going with them.

I need to wake her up. But she looks so damn peaceful. I wonder how she slept in New York. Did she have nightmares?

When she turns over, I get a better view of her face. Her beauty is unlike anything I've seen before. I push up from the chair and walk closer. I can't wait any longer to touch her.

I kneel down next to the edge of the bed as my fingers trail through her hair, pushing the loose strands away from her face. "Zoe, babe, wake up."

She swats an arm out and pulls the blanket up to her chin. "No," she groans. "Go away."

I press my lips to her forehead. "Zoe, wake up," I repeat before leaning on my haunches.

Her eyes snap open, and she stares at me. "Marcel?"

"In the flesh, babe."

"What are you doing here?" she asks.

"I think the better question here is why didn't you tell me you were coming home?" I raise an eyebrow at her.

"I was going to..."

"Yeah? When?" My tone is firmer. I can hear it. But, fuck, I'm little annoyed she didn't fucking tell me. And, honestly, a lot fucking pissed off.

"When I woke up," she snaps back at me, and then her mouth falls open as she scoots back across the bed. As far away from me as she can get. "I'm sorry. I didn't mean that. I didn't mean to... I'm sorry."

"Zoe, if you want to yell at me, yell at me. I can handle it. If you want to chew my ass out for whatever reason, do it. I don't care. I will take you any way you come. Don't think I'm going to break just because you get a little feisty. I'm not that person."

She should know this about me already. But then, I have to remind myself that it's not her fault.

The shit she went through messes with her head. As it would with anyone's.

"I know. I'm sorry."

"Zoe, stop apologising. You haven't done anything wrong." I fucking hate seeing the fear on her face. I hate that she has to second-guess her actions or her words. I want the completely unfiltered version of her. I don't want the person she thinks she has to be.

"I should have told you I was coming home. I don't know why I didn't," she admits.

"Did you not want to see me?" I'm eighty percent sure that she does want to see me, but there's that twenty percent that has me holding my breath, waiting for her answer.

"I did. So much."

I push to my feet and climb in next to her. "I missed you so fucking much," I tell her. My hand wraps around the back of her head and I slam my lips down on hers. Then I kiss her like a man starved. I am one after all. I've gone a month without feeling these lips. Pulling back from the kiss, I lean my forehead against hers. "I fucking missed you so damn much, Zoe. I've been jerking off to the memory of you so much I think I've given myself carpal tunnel."

"Really? Well, I'm back now. What are you going to do with me?"

When I peer up again, I find Zoe smiling wide with lust in her eyes. Her cheeks are rosy and her nipples are hard through the thin material of her shirt. "You want me to show you just how much I missed this body of yours? How much I've been dreaming of sinking into your tight little cunt?"

Zoe lets out a moan, nodding as she says, "Show me."

"Fucking gladly," I grunt, pulling my shirt over my head from behind my back. "Tell me, babe, how much did you touch your pussy thinking of me while you were gone?"

Zoe's face turns bright red and she shakes her head.

"Don't lie to me, Zoe."

"Fine, I might have touched myself once or twice," she admits in a weak voice.

"Just once or twice?"

"Maybe more." Her eyes rake up and down my now naked torso.

Standing up, I undo my belt, then the button and fly of my jeans. I reach into my back pocket, pull out a condom, and place it on the bed. I then proceed to drop my jeans and boxers to the floor, stepping out of them and kicking them aside.

Zoe licks her lips, her eyes drinking me in. "So much better in person," she mumbles.

"Zoe, are you objectifying me?" I laugh before climbing onto the bed.

"I am. But that body was made to be objectified," she says, placing her hands on my chest. "Change of plans... I'm going to show you just how much I missed you." She pushes until I fall backwards on my back.

My breath hitches when she tugs her shirt over her head. She's not wearing a damn thing under it. "Fuck me," I hiss out.

"I plan on it." Zoe smirks, straddling me while her pussy rubs against my cock.

"Oh, fuck." My hands land on her hips, then inch upwards until I reach her breasts. Pinching her nipples between my fingers. Zoe tips her head backwards. Her pelvis grinds down harder, her pussy weeping all over my cock.

"Oh god!" she yells out, her hands resting on my pecs as she lifts her hips slightly. I line my cock up with her entrance and she sinks herself down.

"Fuck, Zoe. Fuck," I hiss out. I know it's been a while, but I don't remember it ever feeling this fucking good. Then realisation hits me. The condom... I'm not fucking wearing it. "Shit, babe, stop." My hand grabs at her hips, lifting her off me.

"What's wrong?" Zoe looks down, concern marring her features.

"Condom," I grit out between clenched teeth while nodding my head toward where the foil packet is still sitting next to us on the bed. "We need a condom."

Chapter Twenty-Two

He stopped me to get a condom...

"Sorry," I mumble, feeling slightly embarrassed. But my attempt to slide off him is short-lived when Marcel's grip on my hips tightens.

"Don't move," he says while reaching for the little foil packet. "This is happening, Zoe. I'm not stopping you for myself, babe. I'm using the protection for you. I don't want you to ever regret being with me. I'd be totally cool with knocking you up—somehow I don't think you'd be as cool with it, though."

"You're worried about me getting pregnant?" I ask him.

"No, I'm worried that you're not ready to get pregnant," he clarifies.

"Oh." My teeth sink into my bottom lip. I thought he didn't want to be with me without protection for his own safety. Maybe because he thinks I'm not clean or something. I mean, I am. I've been checked regularly. Despite what the lab results might say, I've never felt clean. Not since my father sold me into sex slavery.

I shake the thoughts from my head.

"Whatever you were thinking, it's not that," Marcel says before rolling the condom down his length.

"Okay." My eyes stay fixated on his cock. It really is a sight to behold. Thick, long. I think he could have a great career as a dick model. I don't know if that's a thing, but if it is, he could be at the top of the list.

"Babe? You good?" Marcel's question has my eyes moving up to meet his.

"Uh-huh."

His lips tilt up at one side as his hand moves down over my hip, and his fingers glide through the lips of my pussy before sliding into me with ease. "Fuck, you're wet. Is this all for me?"

"Mhmm." I moan as his fingers fill me. Sliding in and out at an excruciating slow pace. "I need you, Marcel."

"You need me? How exactly is it that you need me, Zoe?"

"I need... Oh god!" I lose track of what it is I need when his fingers hit that spot, the one that sets my every nerve ending alight. "I need you inside me, Marcello, now. Please." My head tips back and my hips thrust forward—I'm basically fucking myself on his fingers. Chasing a high I haven't felt in a month.

"I am inside you, Zoe. My fingers are inside you. Fucking you. Would you prefer I fuck you with a different part of my anatomy?" Marcel questions.

"Yes," I moan, while thrusting harder against his hand.

"Yes?"

"I want... oh god... I want... I want your dick

inside me, Marcel. Don't make me beg for it," I cry out.

"You do beg so prettily, babe." Marcel withdraws his fingers, causing me to whimper at the sudden loss. "Lucky for you, I happen to want to fuck you with my cock. So I won't make you beg, Zoe." Marcel fists his sheathed cock. "It's right here, babe. All yours. You want it, take it."

I don't need to be told twice. Shifting my hips so my entrance lines up with the tip of his cock, I slowly sink down. It always amazes me how good it feels when he fills me. It did feel better without the condom. Not that I'm going to tell him that or broach the topic of not using one. I push myself up on my knees and then fall back down, all the way, until I bottom out on him. My hands land on his abs and my fingers trace all the grooves and edges they find there as his body tenses beneath my touch.

"Fuck me, Zoe. You feel so good." Marcel's hips thrust upwards from underneath me. His hands palm my breasts, kneading the flesh. Then he rises up and latches his mouth on to my neck. His teeth graze before they move along my neck, downwards to my shoulder.

My thighs quiver as I continue to move up and down his length, and a light sweat covers my body.

"I'm so..." My words are followed by a moan that echoes through the room.

"Come for me, Zoe. I need to see it," Marcel grunts.

My clit grinds down on his pelvis, circling around and sending pleasure straight through. My nails dig into Marcel's skin as my entire body seizes. I scream his name as I come undone. I must black out, because when my eyes regain focus, I'm on my back with Marcel leaning over me. His fingers running up and down my cheek.

"Welcome back to the land of the living." He smirks.

My brows furrow in confusion. "Did I pass out?"

"Momentarily." Marcel grins. "I've never doubted my abilities. But, fuck, babe, you passing out from pleasure? Best thing I've ever seen. That said, let's not repeat it. You scared the crap out of me."

"It could be your great... abilities. Or it could be the fact I skipped lunch today. I'm jet-lagged and absolutely exhausted," I suggest.

Concern covers his features, and then he's jumping off the bed. "You need food and sleep. Don't move."

"Where are you going?" I ask to his retreating back, his *very naked* retreating back.

Marcel looks at me over his shoulder, a wicked glint in his eye when he notices how quickly I shift my gaze from his ass to his face. "See something you like?" he asks. "I'm going to get you some food, but if you like my ass that much, feel free to take a photo."

"No need for all that. It's not a sight I'll forget in a hurry. Besides, I plan to see a lot more of it in person," I tell him. "Also, there's no food in this apartment."

Marcel walks back towards the bed, where he bends down, picks up his discarded jeans, and pulls out his phone. "I'll order something. What do you feel like eating?"

"Mmm, I'm not sure. You pick something." My hand covers my mouth on a yawn.

Marcel climbs back onto the bed, tugging the covers over me as he does. "Close your eyes. I'll wake you up when the food arrives. Then you can eat and sleep again."

"Marcel?" I look up at him. "Why didn't you tell me about your brother getting arrested?"

His body freezes and his fingers pause on his phone screen. "Who told you?"

"Does it matter? Why didn't *you* tell me?"

"Honestly?" He sets the phone down and pivots

to look at me. "I'm fucking terrified of saying or doing anything that will give you a reason to run from this."

His words hit home. I did this to us. I got scared and ran. "I'm sorry I made you feel like you couldn't tell me things."

"It's not your fault."

"Yes, it is. I gave you a reason not to trust me. I'm flaky. I know that. I want to be better. I want to do this, with you. All in, if that's what you want."

Marcel's smile lights up his face. "I want," he says, cupping the back of my head before he brings his lips down onto mine.

Chapter Twenty-Three

When I tug open Zoe's front door, I'm expecting the Uber Eats delivery guy. What I'm not expecting is to find a couple of pissed off looking Russians staring back at me.

"What the fuck are you doing here?" one of them, Ivan I think, asks.

Folding my arms over my shirtless chest, I smirk and raise one eyebrow at him in question. *Really, fucker? You need me to spell out what I'm doing half-naked in my girlfriend's apartment.* "I could ask you the same thing."

"We're here to check on Zoe. Where is she?"

"Asleep."

"You can either move out of our way, or I'll be more than happy to move you myself," the one I'm certain is Ivan says.

"Try it." I shrug a shoulder, refusing to budge a single step.

"What's going on?" I turn to find Zoe padding barefoot down the stairs with nothing but a thin silk robe covering her body.

"You have visitors," I tell her while slamming the door shut. "You should really put some clothes on before you let 'em in."

"You just opened the door with no shirt on and your pants aren't even done up," Zoe says, trailing her eyes up and down my body.

"Yeah, pretty sure your Russian friends aren't checking me out, babe. You, on the other hand? Well, they're guys and you're hot as fuck. They're most certainly checking you out."

Zoe smiles at me. "You think I'm hot?"

"Insanely,"

"Don't worry, those guys are not checking me out. They're family." Zoe shoves past me and heads towards the door.

"Unless they're blind, they're checking you out," I tell her. Then I lean forward and whisper in her ear, "I can see your nipples through your robe, babe. If they see them too, I'll gouge their eyes out."

Shivers run through her body. Then she turns abruptly. Her hands land on my chest and she pushes me backwards. "I'll be right back," she says before running up the stairs.

By the time I turn around again, the front door is opening and the two fucking Russians help themselves inside Zoe's house like they own the place. They're way too fucking comfortable here. "You find anything on the shooter?" the one who isn't Ivan asks me.

The shooter being the fucker who shot up the restaurant Zoe and I were in a month ago, the same asshole who put a bullet through Dominic's arm. I haven't been able to find out shit about them or who they were aiming for.

At first, I thought it was me, but there's been nothing since the incident. If someone were after me, or any De Bellis, they would have tried again. I've looked into it being an attack on Dom or Lucy too, seeing as both are heirs to well-known billionaire families. I couldn't find anything to suggest the attack was on them either.

There's a small chance it could be random. Some punk-ass fuckers who were bored and thought they'd fill the time by shooting up a restaurant. I highly fucking doubt that's the case, though. I don't believe in coincidences.

"Nothing. You?" I ask, knowing full well they're also looking.

"Nothing. Boss wants her shadowed until we either find them or find out what they were after," Ivan says.

"You think they were targeting Zoe?" My blood goes cold. I've considered the possibility. I'd be an idiot not to have. She's connected to the Pakhan of the motherfucking Bratva. Mikhail Petrov would have a list of enemies a mile long.

Ivan shrugs while offering little more than a noncommittal grunt. I look to the other guy who does much the same.

"Right, I'll find out myself then."

I walk upstairs and find Zoe in the bedroom, where she's pulling a sweater over her head. She's already wearing a pair of jean shorts. "I know I told you to put clothes on. But, fuck, do I prefer you out of them."

"Well, let me find out what they're doing here so I can get rid of them and then you can work on getting me naked again." Zoe leans up on her tiptoes and presses her lips to mine before pulling away from me far too fucking quickly.

"Can I borrow your phone?" I ask her.

"Yeah, it's on the bedside table. Code is one-two-one-three."

"Thanks." I wait until she's halfway down the stairs before I unlock her screen and find the number for the person I'm looking for. I glance at the time and briefly consider not calling. It's a thought that flies out the window as swiftly as I can tap the green button next to his name.

"Zoe, everything okay?" he answers after a couple of rings.

"Petrov, it's Marcel," I tell him.

"Where's Zoe?"

"She's fine. She's downstairs with Dumb and Dumber. What do you know about the shooting that happened before Zoe left for New York?"

"What should I know?" Mikhail answers my question with a question.

"If you know something, then I want to know it too. If there's even an inkling that Zoe's in any kind of danger, I need to fucking know," I growl into the phone.

"Watch your mouth. The only reason you're still breathing is because Zoe wants you to be. Don't make me break her heart by changing that."

"I need to know what kind of danger she's in," I repeat, ignoring his threats that I know are anything but empty.

"If I thought she was in any real danger, I never would have let her go back. My guys are there as a precaution," he says.

"If I find out that someone is after her because of you, there won't be enough Russians in the world to save you," I hiss at him.

Mikhail laughs, as if my words are nothing but a joke to him. Then again, he doesn't know me. "Good talk, Marcello," he says before the call is disconnected.

"Bastard." I throw Zoe's phone down on the bed and head downstairs to find her. It doesn't take long. She's in the kitchen with Mikhail's men. Zoe looks up at me as she bites into a slice of pepperoni pizza. There're two pizza boxes on the counter. No idea where they came from or what's taking our Uber

Eats guy so long to get here, but she's eating so I don't fucking care.

I walk around the counter and stand behind Zoe, wrapping an arm around her waist and pulling her body up against mine. I press a light kiss to her temple while eyeing Mikhail's men, who look anything but impressed by my public display of affection.

Zoe, however, seems oblivious to their scowls. Once her mouth isn't full anymore, she says something in Russian that has the two idiots chuckling. "What'd I miss over the last month?" she directs to them before I can ask her what everyone's laughing about and then she looks to me. "Eat some pizza."

"That isn't pizza, babe. That's fast food's *attempt* at pizza," I tell her as my glare lands on the Pizza Hut boxes.

"It's good, though," she says, taking another bite into her slice.

"Irina left the club," Ivan says, and Zoe gasps. I have no idea who the fuck Irina is so I keep quiet.

"Why'd she leave?"

"No idea. Something about moving onto bigger and better things." Ivan shrugs.

"Huh, maybe I should call her."

"Who is Irina?" I ask Zoe.

"She was one of the dancers at the club. Nice girl."

"You hang out with strippers often?" I lift a questioning brow.

"If they're my friends, then yes," Zoe says. "But so do you. I know you and your brothers own a few of your own clubs around town."

"Owning a club or two and hanging out with strippers are not the same thing," I tell her. "I don't befriend the staff."

"Seriously? You've never once ever *befriended* the staff?" Zoe annunciates the word while wiggling her eyes up and down.

"Not even once," I reply. "Scout's honour. Strippers don't do it for me."

"Were you ever a boy scout? I don't see you being part of group activities."

"Not exactly, but I did my fair share of hunting and knot tying." Probably not the type a boy scout would do.

"Right. Well, thanks for the pizza, guys. But I'm exhausted and going back to bed. You two can show yourself out." Zoe points at the Russians before turning back to me. "You need your shirt before you leave, but thanks for coming over to check on me."

I blink at her. Does she seriously think she's

kicking me out right now? Not fucking happening. "Anytime, babe," I say while following her out of the kitchen. When we make it to her bedroom, I hear the front door shut.

Zoe climbs onto her bed. "I'm sorry I'm not better company. I'm just really tired." She yawns.

"You are the best company even if you're asleep," I reply, walking over before dropping my pants and climbing onto the bed.

"What are you doing?" she asks.

"Getting into bed." I shift to one side and hold my arm out for her. "Come on, lie down with me."

"You want to sleep with me?"

"I always want to sleep with you, Zoe." The hidden innuendo isn't lost on her. Zoe's cheeks turn pink as she rests her head in the crook of my shoulder. My arm wraps around her back. "I'm really fucking glad you're home," I tell her while kissing the top of her head.

"Me too," she says.

Chapter Twenty-Four

S taring at my computer screen, I'm drawing a blank. Lucy and I were working together on the designs for Lobson's bedroom while I was away. But now that I'm back, she's given me full control of the project.

Almost every room in the empty house has been completed. There are only a couple left unfinished.

The main suite being one of them. Even though I should be focusing on my client, my mind keeps drifting to Marcel's bedroom.

I only saw it once. But I remember his dark-timber king-size bed and black sheets with navy coverings. I wonder if he'd let me redesign his room. I mean, there's nothing wrong with it. It's just not very... inviting. It's the kind of space that makes you wonder if you should really be in there or not. Then again, maybe that's intentional. A way to keep people out of his space.

There's a lot that Marcel keeps locked up. Sometimes I wonder if he's trying to protect me, or if he just doesn't trust me enough to let me in. I've been trying not to think about it too much. I've been back a week, and Marcel has been over to my place every night, but he's yet to invite me over to his house.

Do I want to go back there? I'm not sure, but I do want him to *want me* there. My head is all kinds of fucked up when it comes to Marcel. I want more than I should want from him. And with him. I also want more than I know I can actually give him.

Jolting from the shrill tone of my phone, I see Mikhail's name flash on the screen. He's been calling me every day, at least twice since I came back to Melbourne. "Mikhail, don't you have some kind of empire to run? Some toy soldiers to boss around? Babies to tend to?" I ask the moment I swipe answer.

"I do, but I also have a more than capable wife who my soldiers and children seem to listen to more than they do me most days. How are things over there?" he asks.

"Good. Same as they were four hours ago when you called me last." I laugh and spin around in my office chair. "How are things on your side of the world?"

"Would be better if you were still here where I could see that you were safe with my own eyes."

"You have at least four eyes on me. I can see two of your men outside my window as we speak," I remind him. They're trying to be discreet. They stay in their car, parked outside my office. I don't mind. It's like a safety blanket I know I probably don't need but want to hold on to anyway.

"You can never be too safe, Zoe. How's that boyfriend of yours treating you? Can I kill him yet?" Mikhail asks.

"No, you cannot. He's good—oh shit." I jump as a bird flies into the window.

"What happened? Zoe?"

"Nothing. Sorry. It was just a bird." I frown as I

watch that same bird continue to peck at the glass with its beak.

"A bird?"

"Yeah, it's knocking on the window like it's trying to get in. Weird."

"A bird is knocking on your window?" Mikhail attempts to clarify.

"Yeah. Anyway, I should get back to work."

"Zoe, I need you to go and get into Ivan's car. Now," Mikhail says in a more serious tone.

"What? Why?"

"A bird at your window. It's a bad omen. It means death, Zoe. Go and let Ivan take you home. Please."

"Oh my god, not you too." I sigh. "What is it with big bad mafia men and their superstitions?"

"What are you talking about?"

"Marcel... He believes his family is cursed. Even gave me this red bracelet to wear for protection. It's stupid, but I'm wearing it anyway." I laugh. "A bird tapping at my window does not mean death is coming for me, Mikhail. I'm fine."

"Zoe, either you're going to Ivan's car now or he's coming and sitting in your office with you."

"You're being ridiculous. Don't worry so much. I gotta go. Talk to you later. Love you." I hang up before he can argue any more about some bird of death.

Not that it matters. Seeing as it takes less than two minutes before Ivan is barging into my office and sitting on the sofa. "Boss says you got a bird problem." He glares at the window, where there is in fact no longer a bird.

"Boss is just being overbearing," I retort before I pick up the phone and message Lucy. I need to get out of the office.

ME:

Want to meet for drinks?

LUCY:

Always. Where?

ME:

How about that little champagne bar across the street?

LUCY:

I'll meet you there in twenty.

ME:

Perfect.

I'm packing up my things when Ivan stands. "Where are we going?" he asks.

"*I'm* going to the champagne bar across the street. *You're* going back to your car," I tell him.

"Can't do that." He shakes his head at me.

I don't bother arguing with him. It's pointless really. I know I won't win. He's had a direct order from his boss. Which means there's nothing I could possibly say to make him change his mind.

***

Three glasses of champagne later, I'm feeling a lot less stressed. "You know what we should do?" I say to Lucy.

"What?"

"Dance. We should go dancing," I tell her.

Lucy stares at me. "You don't *go dancing*, Zoe."

"Well, there's a first time for everything. Come on, Lulu, take me dancing." I try to pull off a pout, but it only makes her laugh.

"Okay, I'll take you dancing... *if* you stop doing that weird thing with your lip. Let me call the girls. They'll meet us there."

The girls are Lucy's friends. Shardonnay, Xavier's fiancée. And Dani, who works at Xavier's law firm and is dating one of the partner's there. I've met *the girls* a couple of times in passing, but Lucy is right. I don't usually go out. I tend to avoid crowded places.

Right now, though, I couldn't think of anything better than going dancing. I guess all this talk about death birds today makes me want to live it up. "Okay, let's do it." I smile at Lucy.

"Come on, we'll get those big hot Russians of yours to drive us," Lucy says.

Arm in arm, we walk over to the table where Ivan has been watching the entire bar. "We're going to Unhinged," I announce. "Can you drive us?"

"No, you're not," he says firmly.

"Ah, yes, I am. Either you drive us, or I'll get an Uber," I tell him, already pulling up the rideshare app on my phone.

"Fucking hell, you're going to get me killed, Zoe," Ivan grunts before pushing up from his seat. "Let's go."

Lucy and I share a smile as we follow him out of the bar and slide into the back of his car.

By the time we reach the club, Lucy gets a text from Shardonnay. Letting her know they're already in the VIP section. Ivan follows close behind us as we make our way up the stairs and find Lucy's friends in a booth.

I stop, dead in my tracks, when my eyes land on her. Except she looks different from when I met her the first time. Eloise, Marcel's sister-in-law. Guilt consumes me. I accused her husband of hurting her. In my defence, that wouldn't have happened if

Marcel had told me what had happened to her before inviting me over for dinner.

Lucy is oblivious to my discomfort as she slides into the booth, next to a blonde girl who looks anything but pleased to be here. I don't think I've met her before.

"Everyone, this is my friend, Zoe. Zoe, you've met Dani and Shar before. This is El." Lucy points to Eloise, who smiles back at me, then to a girl next to her. "This is Claire and that sad-looking one over there is Daisy," Lucy says while gesturing to the beautiful blonde. "Wait... Why do you look like your cat just died?"

"She's, ah, been secretly not-so-secretly dating Gabe," Eloise announces.

"I thought your brothers-in-law were off limits," Lucy directs to Eloise.

"So did I," Eloise replies.

"Okay, so this has turned into a bit of a De Bellis women gang quick." Lucy laughs.

"What do you mean?" Claire asks her.

"Zoe is Marcel's girlfriend." Lucy points to me. Then all eyes turn my way.

"You're Marcel's Zoe?" Daisy asks.

"Ah..." I look around. I don't know what to say. I mean, I *am* dating Marcel. But clearly he doesn't want me around his family and suddenly I'm sitting with his sister-in-law and his brother's girlfriend. I don't feel like I should be here. "I..."

"Damn, all the good De Bellis men are taken. I mean, if Vin was a few years older, he'd be the best one, but teenagers are not my thing." Dani sighs.

"Dani, you're engaged to be married. You don't need a De Bellis. You have your hot boss," Eloise tells her.

"Yeah, but there's something about that dark and mysterious thing. Am I right? I mean, obviously I'm not giving up hot boss, but still..." Dani shrugs.

I look around the club, feeling really uncomfortable. The buzz from the champagne has worn off, which means I need to either get it back or leave. "I'm just going to the restroom," I tell the girls.

"I'll come with you." Eloise calls out after me. Once we're in the bathroom, she turns. "We didn't have the best first meeting, but let's start over. I'm El," she says while holding out a hand.

I smile. "Zoe. And I'm really sorry about how I behaved at your house," I say, placing my palm in hers.

"Don't be sorry. What you did was brave, and had I been in the situation you thought I was in... well, I would have needed someone like you."

"Still, I shouldn't have jumped to conclusions, and I am sorry I did," I tell her.

"Come on. Let's pee so we can get back out there before another one of my friends tries to claim one of our brothers." She laughs.

I don't miss the way she just included me in her family. I don't even know them. "Can you blame them, though? I mean, I don't know them all, but if they're anything like Marcel, then I can see the appeal."

"I know, right? It should be illegal for one family to have such good genetics. How does that even happen? There's not one ugly duckling amongst the five of them." El laughs.

As we make our way back out of the bathroom, I feel lighter. Like maybe coming here tonight was a good decision.

Chapter Twenty-Five

I've never felt more fucking helpless in my life. Seeing my brother behind bars isn't a pleasant sight. It's a reality I've always known was possible. We don't exactly follow the law in our line of work. Gabe doesn't seem to be fazed, though. He's not concerned about himself at all. Just Daisy. His girlfriend.

I haven't had a lot to do with her personally. I know that Gabe is head over heels in love with the girl. That much is evident to anyone who spends one minute alone with the two of them.

Daisy has been at the house since Gabe got locked up. She doesn't leave her room much, which is why I was surprised to learn that Eloise and Daisy both went to a club tonight. And I laughed my ass off when Gio learned the whereabouts of his wife.

We'd just left the prison after visiting Gabe when Gio got a call from Dan. The guy he's got following El around. About ten minutes later, I got the same call from Vin, who was following Zoe at a distance. She's already got two Russians on her tail. If she knew I was also having her shadowed, she'd have my balls in a glass jar quicker than I could blink.

The last place I ever thought I'd see Zoe was a nightclub, though. I thought Vin was taking the mick when he said Zoe went into Unhinged with Lucy Christianson. Which is why Gio and I are currently on the way to that very same nightclub.

I've been trying to call her. Zoe doesn't like crowds. I don't know why she'd willingly walk into a fucking nightclub. Pulling out my phone, I fire off a text to Dom.

ME:

You know where your fiancée is?

DOM:

I always know where she is. Why?

ME:

You at Unhinged?

DOM:

In the office.

ME:

See you soon.

I don't ask him to check on Zoe. He'll be hiding out, watching both girls through the CCTV footage. I know Dom. He's not about to let Lucy out of his sight for long, especially in a nightclub. The guy has some serious control issues.

"Can this car go any faster?" I ask Gio.

"I'm already breaking every fucking road rule that exists, Marcello." His fingers grip the steering wheel so tight his knuckles are white. Then Gio looks across at me. "You really like this girl, don't you?"

"I love her," I tell him.

"What about the curse?"

"I'm not letting anything touch her." I will fall on my own fucking sword if I have to. I will sacrifice myself before I let anything touch Zoe. Fuck the fucking curse.

"We can't always protect the ones we love," Gio says with a frown. I know he's thinking about his wife, and how she was attacked not long after their wedding.

"I know, but that doesn't mean we shouldn't do everything we can to try. Besides, Zoe is a Petrov. She has more than just the De Bellis family looking out for her."

"That also means she has more targets on her back," Gio points out the obvious.

It's a fact I'm well aware of. I've been searching for a possible connection between Zoe and the shooting at the restaurant. I haven't found anything, but it's odd that nothing has come from it. Like I've said before, I don't believe in coincidences.

"You should bring her back to the house. Let everyone meet her for real. If she's going to be a part of your life, then she's a part of all our lives, Marcel."

"That didn't go down so well last time I tried to bring her around," I remind him.

Zoe ran back to New York the morning after. I'm fucking petrified of doing anything to scare her off again. I've been walking on eggshells all week, almost afraid to do or say anything that could possibly upset her. It's fucked up, and something I need to sort out. It's not her fault. I don't blame her for needing time. She's been through shit no person should ever have to go through. I understand her hesitation. I just don't like it.

Although, since she's been back, she doesn't seem as flighty. She says she's *all in*. That she wants to give us a real go. It's me who's holding back this time, because I don't want to risk not having her.

Gio stops in front of the club and I jump out of the car before he even comes to a full stop. I hear him yell after me but I don't bother looking back. I need to see her for myself. The bouncers open the rope for me without question, as they always do. This isn't my first time at this club. And I head straight for the VIP section because that's Lucy's usual hangout spot.

I climb the stairs and find them straight away. And then I pause. Zoe isn't just sitting with Lucy. No, she's hanging out with Eloise and Daisy as well.

I spot Ivan in the booth in front of them. He clocks me, acknowledging my presence with a nod. I don't know what to do. I want to walk up to the table, take Zoe, and walk the fuck back out again. But then I see her smile. She's happy. She's enjoying herself, and that's not something I'm going to ruin for her.

As I'm standing like a fucking idiot staring at my

girl, Gio barges right past me. That fucker has no qualms when it comes to going in, claiming his wife, and dragging her ass out of here. I follow him over to the table and get there before he has a chance to open his mouth. Sliding into the booth and wrapping my arm around Zoe. Thankful she's sitting on the edge.

"Fancy seeing you all here. Gio convinced me we needed a night out. I tried to tell him he's too old for the club scene but he wasn't having a bar of it." I give her my best easygoing smile.

Zoe's eyes roam all over my face. I have no idea what she's searching for. "Are you... Never mind," she says while shaking her head.

I frown at her, about to ask her to finish her question when Eloise's voice yells out over the noise of the music, "Gio De Bellis, if you're crashing girls' night, then at least be useful and get us a new bottle of champs."

"Oh, more champagne! Yes, that's the best idea I've heard all week." Zoe turns her attention to El.

Leaning in so only she can hear my words, I whisper, "I'm pretty sure you told me the same thing about a third orgasm last night."

Zoe gasps and spins around to face me. Her eyes

wide open. "You can't say that here. In front of people," she tells me.

"What'd he say? I wanna hear." Dani, one of El's friends, chimes in.

"Nothing," Zoe says before leaning in against my ear. "I want to dance."

"Downstairs?" I ask her.

Zoe bites her bottom lip and nods her head. "I think so."

"Let's go." I stand and hold out a hand to her. I don't need a second invitation to dance with Zoe. Having her body pressed up against mine is a fucking daily goal of mine. One I make sure I achieve. "If at any point you want me to get you out of here, say the word and we're gone."

"I'm good. I wanted to come here. I want to dance—even more now that you're here." She smiles back at me.

"Well then, show me what moves you've got, babe." I take Zoe's hand and guide her down the stairs to where the main dance floor is situated. It's full of people, and I have to push through the crowd with Zoe right behind me until I find a spot.

I wanted a darkened section of the dance floor. Somewhere we're not privy to everyone's attention. I plan on making this a dance experience she'll never forget. I can feel the tension coming off her. I don't like seeing her fight with herself for control. So I do the only thing I can think of that will help. Distract her.

Pulling her body up against mine, I press my thigh between her legs and press her as close as I can get her. My arm is tight around her waist.

Zoe gasps, and her hands land on my biceps. "What are you doing?"

"Dancing," I tell her before slamming my lips down on hers. My tongue pushes into her mouth, tasting the champagne on her.

Moving my hands to Zoe's hips, I start circling them, showing her exactly how I want her body moving against mine. I swallow her moans. Her hands tighten on my arms, those nails of hers digging in through the fabric of my shirt. "Oh god. Marcel, stop."

Her words are like a bucket of cold water. My hands leave her body and I take a small step back. "What's wrong?"

"Nothing, I just..." Zoe looks around. No one is paying us any attention. "I was about to come," she whispers.

I smirk. "I know. That was the point of what we're doing," I say while wrapping my arms back around her body. "I want you to come. Right here, right now, Zoe."

"Here. Everyone will see." She gasps again as I press her core against my thigh.

"No one will ever see you. I won't allow it. Trust me, babe. I've got you. Let yourself go, Zoe. I've got you," I repeat, hoping my words sink in. I will always have her.

Zoe's eyes are filled with lust. Her breath hitches as I circle her hips against my body. And then she takes over, moving against me. Her core grinding down on my leg. "Oh shit," she hisses.

My hands cup her face, moving her hair away. "I fucking love seeing you come apart for me. I've never seen anything more beautiful in my life," I tell her.

We don't break eye contact as we dance, and it doesn't take long before Zoe's coming. Her mouth drops open and her body goes rigid in my arms.

"Fucking perfect." I slam my lips back onto hers.

And then, a sound I'm all too familiar with has me pushing Zoe to the ground. My body covering hers as I look around at the chaos unfolding before my eyes.

Reaching towards my lower ankle, I pull the small pistol out I have strapped there. And push to my feet while pulling Zoe up off the ground. All around us, people are screaming, running, barging into each other as gunshot after gunshot rings out through the dark room.

"Stay behind me," I tell Zoe as I start to drag her towards the closest exit.

Chapter Twenty-Six

The grip Marcel has on my hand is so tight I'll probably have bruises tomorrow. My eyes dart around the room, my heart beating out of my chest as I stay as close to his side as I possibly can, following him to wherever he's going.

He lifts his arm and the sound of his own gun firing off shots deafens me. Then a man in a ski mask drops to the floor right in front of us. Before I can contemplate what's happening, my body is being raised and then we're moving. Marcel is running, pushing through the crowd while knocking people out of his way.

Everything happens so fast. A flurry of movements followed by an eerie silence.

My feet hit the ground, Marcel's arm still wrapped around my back. "You okay? Are you hurt anywhere?" he asks, the panic clear in his voice.

I look around the alley. It's quiet out here. I can't hear anything other than the heavy breathing coming from Marcel and my own heartbeat going haywire in my chest. "I'm okay," I manage to get out. "Are you?"

"Let's go." Marcel takes hold of my hand again and starts guiding me towards the back of the building. A door behind us opens and like a freaking ninja, Marcel is in front of me again, his arm outstretched and his finger on the trigger.

Gio approaches us, a terrified-looking Eloise right beside him. "You good?" he asks Marcel, briefly looking at me before diverting his attention back to his brother.

"Yeah, you?" Marcel asks.

"Dan's coming around with the car now," Gio says just as an SUV turns into the alley.

"What the fuck was that?" Eloise questions with a hand to her chest. I can only assume her heart is beating as quickly as mine.

Gio wraps his arms around her and holds her against him. The love he has for his wife is written all over his face. When the car comes to a stop in front of us, Gio swings open the back door. "Get in," he says while ushering Eloise inside. Then he steps away from the door and turns to me. "Your turn. Get in."

I look at Marcel, who nods his head. Then, with a hand on my back, he guides me towards the open door. "It's okay," he says. "We're going to get you home."

I climb inside, expecting him to follow me. What I don't expect is for the door to close and the car to start moving.

Eloise's hands are digging into the leather of the seats as she starts screaming at the driver. "Dan, stop the fucking car. What the hell are they doing?"

"Mrs De Bellis, you need to calm down. The boss has it under control," the driver replies in a soothing tone.

"Has what under control?" I ask him.

"I'm taking you both home. Gio and Marcel will meet you back there," he says.

"No. Let me out of this car." I try to steady my voice. I don't like being locked in, and I like the fact that Marcel is back there even less. What if whoever was attacking that place is still there?

I tug on the door handle but nothing happens. My heart rate picks up. So does my breathing. I can feel the panic building. *I can't do this.*

"Stop the car. Please," I say. "I need... I need to get out." Everything sounds like it's underwater.

Where is Marcel? I need him here. I can't be locked in this car. A hand grips around mine and I turn my head away from the window and towards Eloise.

"You're safe here, Zoe. It's going to be okay. Marcel will probably be back at the house before we even get there," she says while attempting to comfort me.

"No. I need to get out. Stop the car." I scream louder, snatching my hand free then using it to pound against the windows. It's not her fault, and I feel bad when I see her flinch.

Realizing I'm doing little more than making a fool out of myself, I drop my arms, reaching into the bag that I'm thankful was crossed over my body while I was dancing, and find my phone. Then I scroll through the contacts until I land on Mikhail's name.

I don't know where Ivan ended up in all of this mess. But right now, I could really use the familiarity. Before I press the call button next to his name, I hit the number above it. Marcel.

The phone rings, and just as I think it's about to ring out, he answers. "Zoe, what's wrong?"

"What's wrong? Tell whoever is driving this car to stop and let me out, Marcel. I need to get out. Please, let me out." Tears are falling down my cheeks.

"Fuck," Marcel curses under his breath before softening his tone. "Zoe, listen to me. Dan is driving the car. Dan is a good guy. I promise. He's just taking you home. I'm going to meet you there. Wait for me in my room. I won't be long."

"No. I can't. I need to get out, Marcel. I need to... I can't..." I am almost panting by this point.

"Zoe, I can't let you out in the middle of the street. Please, just let him take you to my place. I need to know you're safe, Zoe," he says more quietly.

I can't find the words to respond. I don't know what to say. I should just wait until the car stops and then I can run.

"Zoe, Ivan is here. He's coming to you."

"Ivan is there?" I ask.

"Yes."

"Put him on," I tell Marcel. Ivan will get me out of here.

"Zoe, I'm five minutes behind you. I need you to stay with the De Bellis guy until I reach you."

"You're okay?"

"I'm fine. How are you?" Ivan says.

"I need to get out of this car. They won't let me out," I tell him.

"I know. Just try to stay calm. I'm coming to get you," he says this part in Russian. Words I know all too well, because Mikhail has said them over and over again throughout the years. Whenever I'd have a panic attack, Izzy would call Mikhail and he'd tell her the same thing.

"Okay," I say while taking a huge breath. I try my best to calm myself.

I'm going to be okay. I'm not trapped. Ivan is going to come and get me. And then I can go home.

"Zoe?" Marcel's voice comes back on the line. "I'm sorry."

"It's okay," I tell him. It's not. Nothing is okay. It seems like I can't be in public with Marcel without getting shot at. Either the people doing the shooting have really bad aim, or they're not actually trying to kill anyone.

"It's not. You're not okay and that's my fault," he says.

"Marcel, are you coming?" I ask him.

"I'm on my way. I'll be right behind you, babe."

"Okay." I disconnect the call and drop my phone back into my bag. Then I turn to Eloise, who is watching me with cautious eyes. "I'm sorry," I tell her. "I just don't like being trapped in small places."

"Yeah, me either," she says.

When we pull up to the De Bellis mansion and the gates shut behind us, with four guards standing at it, all of my hopes of getting out and running vanish. And all of my panic and stress about being trapped starts rising to the surface again.

"Come on, I'll make coffee or pour us some wine. Whatever you want," Eloise says when the door opens.

"Thanks." I offer her a tight smile as I follow her out of the car and into the house. "You have a lovely home," I say politely, trying to take my mind off the fact that another mafia family lives here. Ivan will be barging inside any moment. If he said he was coming, he will. I know that. I mentally remind myself of the fact that he's coming. Although one man against the army the De Bellis family has is not going to get me out if they want to keep me in.

Marcel isn't like that. I know him. He's not like that. He's going to come here and he will take me back to my house. I just have to keep repeating that in my head.

I trail behind Eloise until we end up in the kitchen. "Have a seat. I'll be right back," she says, clasping her hands together. I don't miss the way they shake a little. She's good at putting on a brave face, but she's not okay.

I don't call her out on it though. Instead, I sit at the kitchen counter and watch her retreating back. Until the sound of a sliding door opening has me turning around. Vin, the young kid I met out front last time I was here, steps through a second later.

"You came back," he says.

"Not willingly," I retort.

He raises his brows before his eyes lower to where my nails are scratching at my forearm. "You okay?" he asks me.

Am I okay? No, I'm not okay. "I'm not a fan of being trapped," I tell him.

"I heard what happened. At the club. You're not hurt, are you?"

"No." I shake my head.

"I have something that can help if you want," he says.

"Help with what?"

"The anxiety, the fear." Vin shrugs. "I get it. I don't like being trapped either."

"What do you have?"

"Come outside." He steps back through the door. And I don't know why, but I follow him out. There's something about this kid that just calls to me. It's odd. I don't know him, but I feel like I do.

Vin pulls a joint from behind his ear and lights it up, taking a couple of puffs before he hands it to me. My eyes widen. I've never smoked anything in my life. "*This* is what you have?"

"Don't knock it till you try it. Trust me, it'll help," he says, waving the blunt in my direction.

I take it from his fingers.

"If Marcel asks, you didn't get it from me," Vin says as I bring the rolled end to my mouth and inhale.

My lungs fill with smoke, which is quickly followed by me embarrassingly coughing up those same lungs.

"You haven't done this before, have you?" Vin laughs.

"No," I say breathlessly, while trying to recover from my choking fit.

"Shit." Vin shakes his head. "Well, you can thank me later." Vin sits down with his back pressed against the wall.

Following his movements, I lower myself down before bringing the joint to my mouth again, inhaling a little bit less this time. I manage to do so without coughing up my entire lung. Just half of it.

Vin snatches the joint from my fingers. "Give that back before you kill yourself and then cause my demise."

"How will me killing myself cause your demise?" I ask him. I can already feel the tension from my body start to melt away.

"My brother loves you. If you die because I got you stoned, then he's going to kill me," Vin says.

"Ah, no, he doesn't." Marcel isn't in love with me. Is he?

"Live in the land of denial if you want, but it's true. You wouldn't be in this house if he didn't."

I stare out at the immaculate gardens, the world around me suddenly more... everything. "Do you like cake?" I ask Vin as soon as the idea pops into my head.

"Oh god, you're one of those stoners," Vin

groans. "Come on, I'll find you some cake." He pushes to his feet while balancing himself against the wall, then holds out a hand to me.

"Thanks. Think we can get chocolate cake?" I ask.

"Probably." He smiles while pulling me to my feet and then letting go of my hand. I follow him back into the house and into the kitchen.

"Oh, Jesus, Vin, tell me you didn't get her stoned." Eloise sighs the moment she spots me.

"She was stressed. I helped her." Vin lifts a single shoulder. "Don't make a big deal out of it, El."

"I won't have to," Eloise says. "Because your brother will. Marcel is gonna be pissed."

"Marcel is pretty." I smile as I plop down into a chair, my lips curling when I add, "I like him."

Chapter Twenty-Seven

I fucked up. I should have known not to shove Zoe in a car and send her home with people she doesn't fucking know. Of course, she's going to freak out in that situation. I wasn't thinking. I was only acting, hyperfocused on getting her somewhere safe and going after the fucking assholes who seem to have a hard-on for shooting up whatever room she's in.

When I heard the fear in her voice, though, my only thought was getting to her. I should have gotten into that car with her.

As I walk through the house, I can hear them in the kitchen. "Marcel is pretty." Zoe says in a strange whispery voice. "I like him."

I smile at her words as I follow the sound. It takes me two fucking seconds of looking at her and her bloodshot eyes to know why she's sitting here with a look of wonder and peace on her face. Fucking Vin.

"What the fuck?" I ask.

"Marcel. It's you." Zoe jumps off the table she appears to have climbed on top of and runs towards me. My arms wrap around her as her hands roam all over my face. "I was worried about you," she says.

"You were? You don't need to worry about me, babe." I lean forward and kiss her forehead.

"Mmm, I do. Because I like you and that means I have to worry," she tells me. "Oh, cake! Did you bring cake?" Zoe looks up at me with hope twinkling in her eyes.

I turn to my younger brother. "I'm going to kill you," I growl at him. "You got her fucking stoned?"

"Shhh. Don't be mad at him. He's my friend," Zoe says.

"Vin is your friend? Since when?" I ask her.

"Since always." Zoe presses her fingers to the crease between my eyebrows. "You shouldn't frown so much. You'll get wrinkles."

"Zoe, you're stoned." I sigh.

"Is that why I feel so good? Mmm, I should have tried this years ago. You should try it too. Vin, share with your brother. He needs to relax," Zoe says.

"Yeah, I'm fresh out, Z." Vin smirks at me.

"Z?" I question.

"She's gonna be my sister. I get to give her nick-names. Anyway, I've got shit to do. Try not to get shot," Vin calls out before pivoting on his heel and making a quick escape.

"What's going on?" Daisy's voice comes from behind me a few seconds after Vin leaves.

When we walked back into the club, it hit me that Daisy was in there. I felt like shit I didn't think of her sooner. But, in all honesty, I didn't think of anyone but Zoe in that moment. I turned to Gio in a panic and he said that she'd left when Zoe and I went down to the dance floor.

"Hey, I'm so glad you're here." Eloise tugs Daisy into a tight hug.

"What's going on?" Daisy repeats.

"Nothing, come on. Help me make dinner." Eloise takes Daisy's arm and drags her farther into the kitchen.

Daisy was always a happy girl. She used to have a brightness to her. But ever since Gabe got locked up, it's like that light has just been turned off. "Did you see him today?" she asks me.

"I did," I tell her while taking hold of Zoe's hands. To stop them from roaming all over my body.

"Is she okay?" Daisy looks at Zoe, then back to me again.

"Oh, I'm better than okay," Zoe says.

"Vin got her stoned," I grunt.

Eloise and Daisy share a laugh, which has Zoe laughing as well. Am I the only one who doesn't think it's fucking funny that my girlfriend is as high as a kite right now?

"Gio's on his way back, El. You two gonna be okay if I take her up to bed?"

"We're fine," El says. When I don't move, she adds, "Promise."

"Okay, I'll be upstairs if you need anything," I tell them. "Come on." I take Zoe's hand and lead her out of the kitchen.

"Wait," she says while digging her feet into the

ground. "What about the cake?" she asks with such seriousness it's hard for me not to smile.

"I'll bring some up to your room for you," El tells her.

"Oh, awesome. Thank you." Zoe grins.

When I finally get her back to my room, I shut the door and lock it. I don't need anyone barging in. "Zoe, you feeling okay?" I ask as I watch her eyes flick around the room, not really focusing on anything.

"Uh-huh. I'm so good, Marcel. Did you know you're really pretty?" she tells me.

"Pretty?"

"Mhmm. So pretty. Too pretty for me."

"Definitely not too pretty for you, babe."

"I think you're too good for me. Or too bad. I don't know which. But I know I'm not good enough for you, Marcel. I can't be the kind of woman you need." Zoe sits on the edge of the bed.

I walk over and kneel in front of her. "Zoe, you are exactly the kind of woman I need. You are everything I need and want." I take her hands in mine.

Zoe shakes her head. "I'm not okay, Marcel. This is hard. I want to be good for you because I really like you and I don't want to lose you."

"You're not losing me, ever. I'm hard to get rid

of." I smile at her. "Zoe, this is love, not war. You don't need to be anything but yourself with me because you are enough. You don't need to be anything other than you."

"Love?"

"Yes, love."

"Vin thinks you're in love with me." She gives me a sad smile. "I told him you're not."

"You're wrong," I correct her. "I am very much in love with you, Zoe Petrov. So much so that your last name is going to have to change real soon."

"But my name's already changed. To Petrov," she says, sounding confused.

"Zoe, it's going to change to De Bellis when we're married."

"We're getting married?"

"One day we are. I love you, Zoe, and I'm not letting you go."

Zoe blinks as she tries to focus on my face. "I love you too," she says. "So much." Her eyes glisten with unshed tears.

"What's wrong?" I ask her.

"Do you think Eloise is really coming with the cake?"

I laugh. "You really want that cake, huh?"

Zoe nods her head eagerly. "So much," she says.

"Okay, I'll go get it. Hop into bed. I'll be right back with your cake." I pull the blankets down and wait for her to shift her body higher onto the mattress before covering her up. Then I lean forward and gently kiss her lips. "I love you so fucking much," I tell her.

"I love you too. Please don't break my heart, Marcel," she whispers.

"I will protect it with my life, Zoe. I'll keep your heart safe, always," I say and then walk out of the room.

When I reach the bottom of the stairs, Ivan is there arguing with Santo. Not a good scenario for either of them.

"What's going on?" I ask. Both of them turn and stare at me.

"Where is she?" Ivan grunts.

"Sleeping," I tell him.

"I need to see her," he says.

"Yeah, that's not happening. She's fucking asleep," I reiterate. "In bed."

"Boss's orders."

"I don't give a fuck what your boss wants. She's asleep and no one is fucking creeping around her when she is." I already have my phone out of my pocket and am dialling as I'm telling him this.

Mikhail answers his phone. "De Bellis, where's my daughter?"

"She's fine. She's asleep."

"Then why the fuck are you calling me? Shouldn't you be out there looking for the fucking assholes who keep shooting at you?"

"Your boy here thinks he needs to go creep on Zoe while she's asleep. You better tell him otherwise, because I will put a bullet between his eyes before they ever see her in a fucking bed," I hiss down the line.

"First of all, she's not asleep. She's in the hallway upstairs right now."

"How do you know that?" I look back up the stairs. There's no way he can know that. Is there?

"Doesn't matter how. This is the second time she's been out with you and had bullets flying at her, Marcello. There won't be a third."

"They're not after me," I say before sucking in a lungful of air. What I have to say isn't going to go over well.

"What are you talking about?"

"It's her. They're after her," I tell him.

"Why the fuck would anyone be after Zoe?"

"Good question, but the stupid cunt I shot tonight was pointing the end of his barrel at Zoe, not me," I say. "Tell your boy he's not walking into a fucking bedroom to look at my girlfriend." I hang up the call and pocket my phone.

A second later, Ivan's phone is ringing and he's glaring at me as he answers it.

"Santo, follow me." I start back up the stairs.

"You just going to leave this Russian prick here in our house?" Santo growls.

"Yes," I grunt. "Leave him. He's here for Zoe."

"I don't care if he's here for the fucking Pope. Fucker shouldn't be here at all, Marcello," Santo says, catching me halfway up the stairs.

"I need you to check on El. I think she's putting on a brave face, but tonight shook her," I tell him.

"Okay, but you gotta get the Russian out of the house," he throws out over a shoulder as he stomps back down the stairs again.

I find Zoe roaming around the hallway, staring at old pictures on the walls. I look up at the cameras. That fucker has hacked into our security system. I make a mental note to make a major upgrade first thing in the morning. "Zoe, babe, I thought you were in bed."

"Your family has really good genes, you know. There are no ugly ones. Like at all," she says.

"Really? Maybe you need glasses, babe. My

brothers are all butt ugly. You got the best-looking one in the bunch. Trust me." I wink at her.

"Oh, I did. I know that, but they're not ugly." She frowns. "Maybe that's the curse, you know? Someone wanted good-looking children, so they made a deal with the devil."

"That's not the curse," I tell her.

"Mikhail thinks *I'm* cursed," she says.

"What?"

"There was a bird at my window. It means death or something in Russia. It's nonsense of course," she explains while waving a dismissive hand.

"He said a bird at your window means death?"

"The bird tapping at the window is a warning, of death coming. I think he's had one too many vodka shots, if you know what I mean."

"Probably. Come on, let's go to bed. It's late." I take her hand in mine, overcome by this sudden need to hold her tight and not let go.

Chapter Twenty-Eight

I wake up alone in a strange room. No, not a strange room. Marcel's bedroom. He really needs to let me redecorate.

My mouth is so dry. Argh.

I climb out of the bed and head for the adjoining bathroom. After freshening up, I find a new toothbrush in the cabinet and use it to brush my teeth. Trying to erase the awful taste in my mouth. As soon as my teeth don't feel like they have a coating of fur on them, I comb my fingers through my hair before helping myself to Marcels closet. I pull down one of his hoodies and throw it over my head. It's so long it's practically a dress on me.

Then I walk out of the room and head downstairs. I have no idea where he is. And, honestly, it's probably going to take me an hour just to find him in this house. Unless I ask one of the many men standing around. I find one of them at the bottom of the stairs.

"Hey, um, do you know where Marcel is?" I ask.

The guy stares at me like I'm some kind of alien for a full minute before he clears his throat. "Games room. Down that way, third door on the left," he says.

"Thank you," I say, moving in the direction he pointed.

I don't find Marcel in the games room. I do, however, find one of his brothers. Santo. The one I haven't met yet. I've met the other three, although briefly. Santo looks up at me, and there's a deadness in his eyes that takes me back to another time.

"Sorry... I was looking for Marcel," I say, suddenly feeling like I need to flee.

"He'll be back in a minute. You can come in. I don't bite," he tells me.

I walk into the room and sit on the sofa opposite him. "Santo, right? I'm Zoe."

"I know who you are," he says.

Okay, so this is clearly not the friendliest brother out of the lot of them. Where is Vin? I like that one better. I look around the room, trying not to fidget.

"What happened to you?" Santo asks.

My head snaps back to him. "Excuse me?"

"Your skittish as all fuck and you look... Well, broken knows broken. So, like I said, what happened to you?"

Broken knows broken. What the hell does that even mean?

I look at him, really look at him. And for a reason unknown to me, my mouth opens. "My father sold me to repay his debts when I was seventeen. I was auctioned off to the highest bidder and then my body was used against my will over and over again. So if I come across broken, maybe I am. But I have a damn good reason to be."

"Didn't say you were broken without reason. Just that you were," he grunts in reply. "My father beat my fiancée to death, while she was pregnant with our child on the night before we were meant to be married. Guess we're both the result of shitty fucking fathers."

"Guess so." I sigh. "I'm sorry about your fiancée."

"Yeah, me too." He frowns. "Do you think it's possible to know someone your whole life but not really know them at all?"

"Yes, I do," I tell him. "People only show you what they want you to see."

"You're smart," Santo says. "Probably too smart to be with Marcello."

"He's pretty smart too." I shrug.

"Sometimes. But he went and fell in love. And that's just plain dumb."

"Why is it dumb?" I ask him. It's way too damn early for a deep conversation like this, but looking at Santo, I don't think it's early for him. I'd say it's late. I doubt he's been to bed yet.

"Because love is the thing that will end you."

"We're all dying, Santo. We're born to die. Love isn't what ends us. Life is," I tell him. "Love is what makes us live. Love makes everything better, not worse."

"That's because you haven't lost love. And I hope for your sake you never do."

"I don't doubt that you loved her, but have you

ever thought it's possible that maybe there's another love out there for you?"

Santo glares at me. "No," he snaps. "I'm not a cheater. I was fucking loyal. I *am* fucking loyal. Even if she wasn't."

Even if she wasn't? Did his fiancée cheat on him? But that's not a question I'm going to ask him. I'll ask Marcel later.

"Moving on isn't cheating. It's living. You might not be ready for it yet, but one day you're going to meet someone, and I hope when that day comes, you've healed enough to open yourself up to what could be."

"That day isn't going to come. Nice chat, Zoe. Tell Marcel I got tired of waiting for his slow ass." Santo pushes up from the sofa opposite me and walks out of the room.

There's a part of me that wonders if the saying *it's better to have loved and lost, then to never have loved at all* is all just bullshit. Because looking at Santo, seeing the heartbreak written all over him, yeah, I don't ever want to experience that kind of pain.

He's right. I am broken. But even with everything I've been through, I'm not as broken as he is. Maybe it's because I've had time to heal. Time to conceal my scars a little better. Or maybe it's because I found Marcel.

"Hey, I didn't know you were awake," Marcel says, walking into the room almost like I conjured him up somehow. He leans down and presses his lips to my forehead. And I melt into him. It's such a tender gesture. Something so simple, yet it gives me butterflies every time he does it.

"Um, yeah, I was just talking to Santo," I tell him.

"Santo?"

"Uh-huh."

"Look, whatever he said to you, don't listen. He's not himself right now."

"Did his fiancée cheat on him?"

"Shelli? Why would you ask that?"

"Just something he said… It was odd." I lift a single shoulder into a half shrug.

"What did he say?" Marcel asks while avoiding my question.

"Something about him being loyal even if she wasn't. It just caught me off guard."

"She did, but we didn't think he knew," Marcel says. "We found her journals. And, well, they're… descriptive."

"Why wouldn't you tell him? Show him?"

"Because he's already devastated. He doesn't need to lose her twice," he says.

Maybe Marcel is right, but knowing the truth might also free him in a way as well. I don't know for sure. I mean, I haven't experienced the kind of loss he has. I guess no one really knows how they would react until they have to experience it.

"Did you have any plans today?"

"It's Saturday. So, not really."

"Good, it's family barbie day," he says.

"Barbie day?"

"Barbecue. You know, sun, backyard, beers, meat on the barbecue."

"Oh, a grill out. You guys do that?" I ask him.

"Why wouldn't we?"

"I don't know. I just... I guess with all the suits and serious grumpiness wafting off you and your brothers half the time, I didn't see you as the grill-out type." I shrug.

"You're in for a treat, then. And I'm not grumpy. Gio definitely. But me? I'm the easygoing brother."

"I actually think that Vin might win the title for easygoing brother." I smile.

"You need to stay away from Vin. He's a bad influence," Marcel grunts.

"Too bad. He's the brother I like the most so far,"

I admit. "Do you think we can stop by my place so I can change?"

"I had Ivan get you some things. You've got a bag in my room. *Our* room. You're staying with me for a bit."

"What?"

"I just thought that I spend basically every night at your place. So it's time for you to spend some time at mine," Marcel says, but he's not looking me in the eye.

"What aren't you telling me, Marcello?"

"I want you here because it's safer. We have this place locked up tighter than Fort Knox. No one can get to you here."

"Why would someone want to get to me?"

"I don't know. But I'm working on finding out. These shootings aren't random, Zoe."

"I know that, but I thought... I guess I thought someone was targeting you."

Marcel shakes his head. "I wish they were."

Someone is after me? My hands start to shake. I can feel my heart rate picking up speed.

"Hey. It's going to be okay. I'm not going to let anything happen to you."

"I don't want anything to happen to you either. I just... I want it all to stop. I want to wake up and not even know the mafia world is real."

"You don't really want that. This world is your family, Zoe. The Petrovs, the Valentinos, *me*. We're your family."

"It's not safe, Marcel."

"Life isn't safe, babe. We're all born to die eventually. But you and I? we're going to live a long time. We'll die of old age. You'll probably get tired of me after about sixty years and stab me to death or something."

"That's not funny." I laugh. "I wouldn't stab you. It's too messy, remember? And I'll be old and weak. I'll just poison your food instead."

"When we get our own place, I'm hiring a chef. You are never going in the kitchen," Marcel replies with wide eyes.

Chapter Twenty-Nine

I peer down at the sleeping beauty in my bed and don't want to leave. I have to. This family has too much fucking shit going on not to get up and get moving. But I could easily say fuck it all, pick Zoe up, and just run away with her. I want to take her somewhere far away from all this bullshit.

If I could get away with it, I'd wrap her in bullet-proof clothing and then add some bubble wrap on top just for added protection. The Petrov family has been trying to identify whoever the fuck is after her. All we know about the one dead body left behind at the club was that the fucker was Italian.

He was nothing but a foot soldier for whoever the fuck he's working for, though. No identification. His fingerprints aren't in any databases. Right now, I have his image running through facial recognition software, although that could take days before it brings back a hit.

Zoe's going to want to go to work today. I know I can't keep her locked up forever. Santo volunteered to go with her, which shocked the fuck out of both me and Gio. Santo has been hellbent on keeping women away from the family ever since Shelli was killed. He's been different with Zoe, though. I was watching him over the weekend. He likes her. Not that he doesn't like Eloise or Daisy, but there's something about Zoe that my brother connects with.

I'm not going to question it. If my girlfriend is the key to getting through to Santo, then I'll take it. I'm desperate to get my brother back. At the moment, it feels like my family is being torn apart at the seams. Gabe's locked up, and the longer he stays there, the more my hopes of him getting out diminish.

I can see Daisy losing hope as well. It doesn't help that Gabe has taken her name off the visitation list. She can't even go and see him. She's holding out for the trial though. After that, I'm not sure what she'll do. He could be locked up for years if all the charges stick.

The fuckers wanted him to turn on Gio. That'd never happen. None of us would ever turn on the other. It's the one thing that's unbreakable. Our loyalty, our bond. Trust me, our father tried it more than once over the years. He couldn't stand our brotherhood. He wanted us to hate each other as much as he hated us.

"Babe, I have to go," I whisper into Zoe's ear while pushing her hair away from her face with my fingers.

"Mmm, where?" she groans while slowly blinking her eyes open.

"I have to go see Gabe," I tell her. "Santo is going to take you to your office this morning. Don't give him too much hell." I pepper her face with kisses.

"I don't need a babysitter, Marcel."

"I know you don't. It's for my peace of mind. Just go with it for me. I love you," I tell her.

"I love you too. I'll let Santo come with me, but he's going to be so bored," she says.

"He'll be fine. He likes you."

"I doubt he likes anyone," Zoe grumbles.

"That's not true. He likes me and he likes you. I'll call you later," I tell her, forcing myself to get off the bed.

"Okay. I'm just going to sleep a little longer," she says before rolling over.

I watch her for a second. Then I gently close the door and go in search of Gio, finding him in his office. "You ready?" I ask him.

He looks up from his desk with a glare aimed my way. "Yep," he says, pushing his chair back and standing. "Xavier is meeting us there."

I don't utter a word until we're in the car, away from all the prying ears inside the house. "What are his chances, really?"

"They're not good," Gio grunts, cursing under his breath as he slams his fists down on the steering wheel. "Fuck." It's not often my brother loses his composure. It takes a lot to rattle him. "He shouldn't fucking be there. It should be me," he says.

"We know this is the reality of what we do. Gabe knew the risks. This is the life."

"Maybe it's time to get out of the life..."

"And do what?" I ask, honestly curious. I know there is no getting out of this life, not for Gio, and not for me. I could see Gabe moving on to a more legit role once he gets out. I was supposed to be studying business to run that side of the family empire. Which I'll do, but I don't mind getting my hands dirty either.

"Fuck knows. I just need the family to get back on track. It feels like we're dealing with one hit after the fucking other at the moment."

"I know." My mind drifts to Zoe and finding the fuckers who are after her. I won't rest until I know they're no longer a threat.

"What's going on with Vin?" Gio asks.

"What d'you mean?" I shrug, doing my best to play dumb. I know that Gabe talked to our youngest brother. He didn't elaborate but I don't need him to. There's no good reason for the kid to know about that house our father was keeping behind our backs.

I knew the man was a sick bastard. But that? What Gabe and I found in that house while looking for intel on the old man's secret contacts? That was a whole new level of fucked up. Our father, along with one of his disgusting friends, was running a child sex ring.

Boys and girls as young as ten were locked up in rooms, where they were used against their will. Gabe and I shut that shit down quick. As for the fucker who was running the show, well, we made sure he was no longer able to do shit. But Vin... I can't bring myself to imagine what he was doing in that house, what our father made him do...

That's not my story to tell, though. The kid doesn't want people knowing. I get that, and unless I think he's not coping, I'll take that knowledge to the grave with me. Besides, Gio doesn't need that on his shoulders as well. He'll blame himself, like Gabe and I have been doing since we found out.

It's the only reason I haven't put a stop to the pot. We don't tolerate drugs by any means. But at the moment, I think the kid needs it. It's fucked up, and I shouldn't be okay with my little brother using drugs to ease his mind. At the same time, it's only pot. Anything else and I wouldn't be sitting idly by watching him self-medicate.

"Something's bugging him lately. You think it's all the changes? Something happening at school?"

"He's seventeen, Gio. He's a moody teenager. You were one once too. I know it was a lifetime ago, but you were." I laugh.

"Fuck off. I'm not that much older than you," he grunts.

"Is that a grey hair?" I reach up and touch the side of his head, where there isn't a single grey to be seen.

"Fuck you. There's no grey. And even if there were, it'd be because of you four fuckers stressing me the fuck out."

"Imagine when you and El have your own kids. What's that gonna be like if you're this stressed over your brothers?"

"Our kids will be angels, just like their mother," Gio says with a smile.

"Or they'll be girls and hot, *just like their mother*." I laugh at the glare Gio sends my way.

"I'll buy a farm. Move them out to the middle of nowhere. Or I'll build a town where no boys are allowed to live within a hundred kilometres."

"Yeah, let me know how that works out for you." I shake my head. No way in hell would El let him do all that.

"I'm thinking of moving out," I tell him. "I think it's time."

"You're not moving out," Gio grunts. "Have Zoe move in with you at our house."

"It's not about her. It's just time."

"No, it's not. This isn't the time to be separating. We need to stick together," he says.

"It's not separating. It's moving out."

"Same thing. I can't fucking protect you if you're spread out all over the city."

"Gio, it's not your job to protect us from everything."

"That's exactly what my job is, Marcello. You're not moving out," he repeats like his word is final. In a lot of situations, it is. Except right now. I've already decided on this. I'll have Eloise find me a house nearby, but I *am* moving out.

When we arrive at the jail, we go through the process of getting through to the visitation room. This is the part that always hits me hard. Seeing my brother cuffed while he's forced to parade around in a fucking dark-green tracksuit.

"Hey." Gabe nods at us. His face is healing from a beatdown he took when he first got here.

"How you holding up?"

"How's Daisy?" It's always the first question he asks us.

"You'd know for yourself if you let her come and see you," I remind him.

Gabe glares at me. "Don't fuck with me, Marcello. How is she?"

"She's okay. Still holding out hope you're getting out," I tell him.

Gabe shakes his head. "It's going to hit her hard when that doesn't happen."

"Then put her name back on your visitation list," I groan.

"I don't want her here. This isn't the place for her. Would you let your woman come here?" he counters.

I picture Zoe. And truth is... there's no fucking way I'd want her near a prison. I get his point. It doesn't mean it's right though.

"Should we talk business? Or call doctor Phil for a family counselling session?" Xavier asks.

An hour later, our time is up and I have to walk away. Leaving my brother behind in this fucking hellhole. "I fucking hate this," I tell Gio.

"Yeah," he says while nodding his head in agreement.

Chapter Thirty

It's strange having so many people around me. I'm used to working alone. Or at least having Mikhail's guys stay outside. Now, not only do I have Ivan *inside* my office, I also have Santo.

I could literally cut the tension in here with a knife. The two don't seem to like each other. And honestly, if I had to put money on it, I think Santo would come out the victor if they went at it. I don't know what it is, but he just seems the most unhinged.

"I'm getting coffee. You want something, Zoe?" Ivan asks, pushing up from the small office chair he's been occupying for the last two hours.

"No, I'm good. Thank you." I smile at him.

I'm really not good. I've been trying to pretend they're not here. I've been acting like I'm going through the motions of working, but it's really damn hard to concentrate with an audience. Like I said, I'm used to working alone. I like being alone.

When the door closes behind him, Santo clears his throat, causing me to look up at him.

"What?" I ask him.

"What's wrong with you?"

"You want the full list? I don't think there's enough time in the day for that."

"Why are you making us sit here while you pretend you're working when you're not actually doing anything?"

"I'm trying to work. It's hard with you both in here." I sigh.

"Why?"

"Because it's weird."

"Just pretend we're not here." He shrugs.

"That's not easy." I rub at my temples.

"Why don't we take a lunch break? You look stressed."

"I'm not stressed. I'm... I don't know what I am, but I'm not stressed," I tell him.

Ivan walks back in with a to-go cup of coffee in his hand. I glance in his direction before a sound at the window has me turning that way instead. I frown as my glare lands on the outside ledge. The bird's back.

"Fuck. We need to get out of here," Ivan says.

"Not you too," I groan while spinning back around in my chair.

"What?" Santo questions.

"It's just a bird, Ivan, not an omen," I tell him. "You guys need to cool it with all this superstitious shit."

"What's a bird an omen for?" Santo asks me.

"Mikhail claims it means death is coming. Like I said, it's just a superstition."

Santo looks from me to Ivan before pushing to his feet. "Bring the car around. We were just about to go for lunch anyway. Come on, Zoe."

"Be out front in two minutes. Do not let her out of your sight." Ivan points to Santo, who offers him a mock salute in return.

"Wouldn't dream of it."

"Come on, not you too."

"I'm hungry. Let's go eat," Santo tells me, taking my bag from my shoulder and putting it over his.

"You believe the bird thing, don't you?" I sigh.

"It's not that I believe it. It's just that I don't *not* believe it. Besides, if I ignore it and something happens to you, Marcel's heart will break and I don't want any of my brothers to experience what I have."

"You're right. Let's just play on the side of caution. Why don't we go back to my place for lunch? We can order something and have it delivered?" I suggest.

"Sounds good." As we're walking out of the office, Santo sticks really close to my side. He opens the back door of Ivan's car before climbing in after me.

"We're going to my place. Ordering in," I tell Ivan.

"Sure," he responds, already pulling the car out into traffic.

I smile when my phone rings and I see Marcel's name on the screen. "Hey."

"Hey yourself. Where are you going?" he asks.

"Are you tracking me?" I question him.

"Yes, now, where are you going?" he says as if

tracking someone's movements is a completely normal thing to do.

"To my place. Your brother needs food," I tell him.

"He can fend for himself. You don't need to cater to him, Zoe."

"I know. What are you doing?"

"I'm heading to your place now. I'll be there in five," he tells me.

"How was Gabe?"

"Good. I'll see you in a few," Marcel says before disconnecting the call.

"Okay then," I say out loud. I stare at my phone for another second, then quickly pocket it.

"Don't take it personally. We've been trained not to say too much over the line. It's ingrained," Santo tells me.

That actually explains a lot. At the start, Marcel was hesitant to share too much. Now, though, he tells me as much as he can. I'm sure there's still a lot he doesn't say and that's okay. Because honestly, I don't need to know everything he and his brothers do.

"Marcel is meeting us at my place," I tell Santo.

"You okay?" His eyes seem to sear into me. It's as if he can see right through me. It's weird.

"I'm okay. Are you?" I ask him.

"I haven't been okay for months. But I'm dealing with it," he says.

"I haven't been okay for years," I whisper. "But I'm dealing with it too." I look at Santo before gesturing between the two of us. "Are we becoming friends? Is this what this is?"

"Friends? Family? I don't know." He shrugs. "Do the memories ever fade?"

I shake my head. "They don't. But they become easier to see."

"She would have liked you. Shelli, I mean. I think you guys would have been friends," he says.

"Maybe. I'm kinda hard to be friends with."

"I don't think you are. Besides, you won over Marcello's icy heart. That in itself is an achievement."

I smile. "I don't think you win people over. I think that when you fall in love, it just happens and there's nothing either person can do to avoid it. Like you just see someone. And before you know that it's love, you feel it."

"I don't believe in love at first sight."

"You didn't love Shelli at first sight?"

"We were teenagers when we met. It was lust for sure, but love? That developed over the years," he says.

I have a feeling that, although there's no doubt that Santo loved Shelli, she wasn't his real true love. The kind that changes your entire life. I think that is still coming for him. Of course, I'm not stupid and keep these thoughts to myself.

Ivan stops at the front of my building, where Marcel is leaning up against the wall waiting for us. "Thanks," I say, moving to open the door.

"Wait... I'll get it," Ivan says, cutting the ignition before jumping out on the driver's side.

Santo is next to me. He gets out on the other side of the car when Ivan opens my door. Just as I'm about to climb out, Ivan slams the door shut again and then blood splatters all across the window. His blood. His lifeless eyes meet mine right before his body falls.

I hear screaming. My own screaming. And then I remember Marcel is out there.

No, no, no. This is not happening.

I slide across the seat and push out Santo's door. I don't think of anything but getting to Marcel as I round the car. That's when I stop. He's on the ground too. Santo is holding a hand against his brother's chest. There's so much blood. I look to my right and see Ivan, and then my feet finally decide to move again.

I need Marcel. I need to get to Marcel. This isn't happening.

I take one step towards him when something hits the back of my head. Pain radiates through my skull, my vision blurs, and I feel arms wrap around my body. And then everything just fades out.

Chapter Thirty-One

A sharp pain radiates through my abdomen as consciousness starts to seep in. Blinking my eyes open, I'm blinded by bright lights, the smell of antiseptic, and a god-awful sound of machines beeping.

"Marcello, thank fuck," Vin says. I turn my head to look at him as I try and fail to sit up.

"What happened?" I ask at the same time I remember exactly what happened. I was waiting for Zoe outside her apartment building. She'd just pulled up when we were ambushed out of fucking nowhere. Five guys in ski masks propelled down from the fucking rooftop.

Ivan, who was opening Zoe's door, just managed to shut her back inside the car before he took a bullet to the head. I remember drawing my own gun and firing off a few shots. I got two of the assholes before I felt a burning sensation in my chest.

"Fuck. Where the fuck is she?" I yell, forcing my body upright, not caring about the pain currently tearing through me.

"Lie the fuck down before you rip something and bleed out," Vin hisses.

"Fuck off. Where the fuck is Zoe?" I yell at him while ripping the IV out of my arm.

"That's a question I'd like to know as well." The thick Russian accent has both my brother and me turning towards the door to see Mikhail, the Pakhan of the Petrov Bratva.

I don't bother answering him as I turn back to my brother. "Where's my phone?"

Vin reaches over and picks it up from the table next to the bed. "Gio and Santo are looking for her."

"Where the fuck is she? She was in the car." I don't know who I'm asking at this point. I log into my phone, bring up the GPS tracking app I have, and click on her name.

"She got out of the car. Santo said she was coming to you when they grabbed her. Threw her into a van before he could get to her," Vin explains.

"No." My voice is quiet. "This isn't happening." My eyes stay focused on the app as the circle of death keeps circling. After a few more seconds, it brings up a map with the red dot location of Zoe's phone. "Where are my clothes?"

"Where do you think you're going?" Vin asks, folding his arms firmly over his chest.

"I'm going to get my fucking girlfriend. Either you're helping me or you're not," I growl at my brother.

"Where is she?" Mikhail asks.

I zoom in on the map and take a screenshot of her location before turning it around and showing him. "The docks," I tell him, limping my way around the bed.

"You're in no condition to be going after anyone," Mikhail snarls at me. "If you did your fucking job and protected her like you were supposed to, she wouldn't be in the hands of a goddamned psychopath right now."

"What do you know? Why have they gone after her?"

Mikhail doesn't answer me. He just pivots and walks out of the room. I call Gio as I'm slowly making my way out of the hospital in a fucking gown with my ass on full display. Right now, I don't fucking care. All that matters is getting Zoe back.

"Vin?" Gio answers my call.

"Wrong brother. Where are you?"

"Warehouse district. What the fuck are you doing, Marcel?" he grunts.

"Going to get my girlfriend. I'm sending you her location now."

"How do you know where she is?" he asks.

"Because I installed a tracker on her phone like any good fucking spouse would. Meet me there."

"Stay in the fucking hospital. Santo and I will go get her," Gio says.

I disconnect the call and continue through the hospital at a fucking turtle's pace. "Get me some pain meds," I call over a shoulder to Vin. "Meet me out front."

"Already on it," he says, pulling out a bag of pills

from the pocket of his jeans. I don't ask what they are before I take two of them.

I'm surprised to see Mikhail standing at the front of the hospital, yelling into his phone in angry Russian. I have no idea what the fuck he's saying nor do I care. I have one goal right now, and that's to get to Zoe before it's too late.

"Wait," Mikhail yells at me as I'm walking past him. "Get in the fucking car." He nods towards his waiting vehicle.

"Why?"

"Because if anything happens to you—anything else—Zoe's not going to get past that. So get in the fucking car if you want to help me get my daughter and wife back."

I still. "They have Izzy?"

"No, she fucking went to them willingly," he growls before shoving past me. He climbs into the front of the car.

I look to Vin and shrug as I walk over and gingerly manoeuvre myself into the back. "Why would they want your wife?"

"Why do fuckwits want anything? Money, power, revenge. Take your pick. It doesn't matter. They won't be breathing long enough to get any of it," Mikhail snarls as the car takes off.

A Sinner's Virtue

.   .   .

Chapter Thirty-Two

Something splashes across my face, forcing my eyes open. It takes a lot of effort to get my vision to focus. Everything is blurry. My hand comes up and rubs over my face, wiping the water away.

"Good. You're up. About fucking time," a gravelly voice calls out.

My head pounds. It feels like a thousand jack-hammers are going off inside it. Tiny little men just hammering away. Doing their best to torture me. And then, like a lightning bolt, an image flashes in my mind.

Marcel. He was on the ground. There was so much blood. He wasn't moving. And Ivan. He was...

Tears prick my eyes as the harsh voice yells at me again. "Get up."

I don't move. I can't. All I can think about is Marcel. He's gone. Because of me. I can't... My chest heaves as my lungs struggle to fill with air.

"What the fuck? Get the fuck up now, before I make you."

I don't care anymore. About what he says or what is happening to me. There is nothing they can do to me that matters. If Marcel is gone, then I want to go with him. Let this guy end me. I don't know what he wants and I don't care. I just want it to end.

I knew I was pushing my luck by getting involved with Marcel. Falling for him. Santo was right. Love is a one-way street that leads you right to heartbreak. My chest hurts. It hurts so bad. I thought I knew pain. I thought I'd seen the worst of the worst. I was wrong.

Losing Marcel, seeing him die because of me.

There is nothing that could possibly happen that's worse than that. Which is why when this guy, whoever he is, starts yelling commands at me, I choose to ignore him.

I've been here before. My compliance is irrelevant. I know that he's going to do whatever he wants with me no matter how much I beg or try to get my way out of this situation. You can't reason with a monster. And this monster... he killed Marcel.

He. Killed. Marcel.

My eyes squeeze shut as a sudden bout of anger builds within me. A small ember at first, an ember that's very quickly ignited into a flame, and the burning heats something else in me. A rage so feral I can feel my entire body shaking.

"I'm going to kill you," I hiss at the guy.

"Yeah? You and what army? Look around. There's no one here to save you," he says. "Yet. But that's going to change."

He holds up a phone and snaps a photo of me. "What are you doing?"

"Just giving someone a little incentive." He smirks.

"Who?"

The guy doesn't bother answering me before he presses a few buttons on the phone and then brings it to his ear. "Isabella Valentino-Petrov. You're a hard woman to get a hold of." He winks at me, pulling the phone away from his ear so I can hear Izzy yelling threats through the speaker.

"No, Izzy, don't! Stay away!" My scream earns me a slap across the face, knocking me backwards. My head hits the wall. "No. Leave her alone." I push myself up to my feet and charge forward.

The guy's hand wraps around my throat, and he slams my body back against the wall again. "You hear that, Isabella? That's the sound of your little friend here dying. Come alone, and if I were you, I'd hurry."

"Why?" I gasp, falling to the floor when he releases his hold on my throat. "Why are you doing this?"

"Why? That's a good question. You know, I don't plan on keeping you alive longer than necessary," he says, and that's when I notice his thick Bronx accent.

"I don't care," I tell him honestly. "Leave Izzy alone. Just kill me."

"You aren't the key piece here, sweetheart. You're just a pawn on the chessboard. No, I want the queen. It's always been about her. I want her to suffer like she's made me suffer. She took from me, and now I'm going to take from her." He sounds almost... sad. Not that I feel any kind of remorse for this asshole. I just need to keep him talking long enough for me to figure out a way to kill him. I won't let him hurt Izzy, or anyone else for that matter.

"Why her? What did she take?" I ask him.

"She killed my father," he yells before he starts pacing the small room. I have no idea where I am, or how far away everyone else is. All I know is that this guy is as unhinged as they come and I need to see him dead before I take my last breath.

He claimed Izzy killed his father. If that's true, then I have no doubt the man had it coming. I'm more than aware my adoptive mother has a past. One that involved her earning herself the nickname the *Stiletto Killer*. Something she doesn't do anymore. Which means I also know she only ever killed men involved in the child sex trade. It was how she came to find me.

"I know what you're thinking. That he deserved it. That she must have had a reason."

I watch as he walks back and forth. I don't think he's talking to me at this point.

"He was a good man. He had flaws but so does everyone. He was my father and she killed him."

"Why?"

"Why? Because she's an evil bitch who needs to

be stopped and I'm more than happy to be the one to do it." He stops walking, turns on his feet, and smiles at me. "She's coming for you. I've been watching. I know she's coming for you."

"No," I say, shaking my head. "She won't."

When the sound of tyres travelling over gravel breaks the growing tension, the guy rushes towards the door. "Our little guest is here," he says with a chuckle before stepping out of the room. "Don't go anywhere."

I push up to my feet and run towards the door but it closes and locks before I reach it. My fists pound on the wood. "No. Stop. Let me out!" I scream as I continue to bang on the door, only stopping when I hear voices on the other side.

"No, God, please no. Don't do this," I cry out the moment recognition hits.

The knob turns and then I'm falling backwards at the same time the door is being pushed open. I manage to catch myself and not fall to my ass this time. I shuffle aside, my stomach dropping when Izzy steps into the room with a gun pointed directly at the back of her head.

Why did she come? Why would she put herself at risk for me?

"You okay?" she asks.

I nod my head. Even if I know I'm never going to be okay again. Not without Marcel. "I'm sorry," my voice croaks and my eyes sting with unshed tears.

Izzy smiles at me. It's the same smile I've seen a thousand times over. The one that tells me everything is going to be okay. That everything is fine. The smile that says she has this handled. Although, for once, I think she's wrong.

I don't think this is a room either one of us is escaping. Her three babies are going to grow up without a mother because of me. Mikhail is going to lose her. He lost one of his best guys already. All because Ivan tried to help me.

"Get over there. Both of you," the guy hisses while pushing on Izzy's back.

My adoptive mother doesn't drop her smile, though. She has a wicked gleam in her eye as she turns around, somehow managing to block half of my body with her own.

"Izzy, don't do this. I'm so sorry," I whisper.

"You know, Kevin, when I heard you were looking for me, I didn't think you'd go to such elaborate measures to track me down," she says.

"You know who I am?" The guy appears taken aback.

"Kevin Geraldson II, son of Kevin Geraldson I,

who's waiting for you in a special corner of hell I'm sure."

"You killed him. You took my father. Now I'm going to take something you love. And then I'm going to kill you."

"There are a few problems with your plan," Izzy says calmly. *How the hell is she so calm right now?* "First, I'm not about to let you harm this girl any more than you already have. Second, many people have tried and failed to kill me before. So what makes you think you'd be any better at it?"

"I'm the one holding the gun, bitch." Kevin waves his weapon in the air.

Izzy takes a step towards him, quickly closing the distance between them and then her hands are swiping out. A loud blast pierces through my ears within seconds, and that's when I realise Izzy is the one holding the gun now. The next thing I hear are the guy's screams. There's blood pouring out of his legs as he collapses to his knees and then his laid out on his back.

"Like I said, many have tried and failed." Izzy stalks forward and stands over the guy rolling around on the ground. "You got cocky, Kev. Where are all your masked men now? You thought you could let them all go, and that was your fatal mistake." Izzy pulls the trigger, sending another bullet straight through Kevin's abdomen.

"Fuck you, bitch," he screams at her.

I can't stop staring at the blood. There's so much blood. Too much blood. Visions of Marcel on the ground hit me, and I fall to my knees.

"Your first mistake was thinking you could come after me or my family," Izzy says and then the gun fires off again.

There's a commotion in the room. People are running in. I know I need to get up. I need to help her, but I'm frozen to the spot. I can't move.

Chapter Thirty-Three

I'm right behind Mikhail. Rushing the building. We both start running at the sound of gunshots. Mikhail yells something in rapid Russian before shouldering his way into the room.

"You're late, as always, love." Izzy smiles at him.

My eyes flick around until I spot a guy bleeding out on the ground, bullet wounds littering his motionless body. And then I see her. Zoe. She's huddled on the floor, her back leaning against the wall. Like it's the only thing holding her up.

"Fuck. Zoe." I drop down in front of her. My hands cup her cheek. "Zoe, it's okay. It's going to be okay."

Her eyes are looking directly at me, but they're also not. It's like she's not here. She blinks, "Marcel?" My name is nothing but a whisper on her lips. And then she smiles.

"Yeah, babe. It's me. It's going to be okay," I tell her.

"I know," she says before her eyes roll back in her head. Her body starts slipping to the side, and the next thing I know, she passes out.

"Fuck," I curse under my breath, catching her before she hits the ground. My body tears open with the movement. Literally. I feel the stitches fucking break away from my skin.

"Marcel, move. I've got her." I look up at Santo. My eldest brother is right beside him.

"Come on. We need to get you out of here. You need a fucking doctor. Again," Gio says.

"No." I shove his hands off me and reach out for Zoe, who Santo is effortlessly picking up off the ground.

"I'm just going to carry her out to the car, Marcel. Come on," he says.

I let Gio help me up to my feet. "Fucking hell," he grunts, his eyes landing on the front of the hospital gown I'm still wearing. Which is now covered in blood. Gio shrugs out of his jacket and wraps it around my shoulders. "Come on, let's go," he says while circling an arm around my waist.

I lean my weight on him, moving to exit the room. My eyes focused on Zoe and nothing else.

"Hand her over." Mikhail steps in front of my brother, blocking his path.

"Yeah, that's not happening," Santo snarls at him.

Mikhail tilts his head ever so slightly, an amused smile on his face. I don't think he's used to people telling him no. "I won't ask again," he says.

"Good, I won't answer again," Santo counters.

"Follow us to our place, Mikhail. She needs a doctor," I tell him.

"So do you. Fucking hell, Marcello, what were you thinking?" Izzy asks while throwing a hand out towards my chest.

"I was thinking some psychopath had my girlfriend," I grunt. "Can we talk about this later? She really needs a fucking doctor."

"Let's go." Izzy places a palm on Mikhail's chest. "Come on," she tells him.

Reluctantly, Mikhail turns and exits the room, my brothers and I following right behind him. Izzy and Mikhail argue the whole way out of the building. But all I hear is the last bit as we all reach our respective cars.

"Yeah, well, she loves him, which means we have to tolerate him at best," Izzy tells her husband.

The memory of Zoe and I exchanging those words hits me. She's going to be okay. She's still breathing. Her heart is still beating. She's going to be okay.

Gio helps me into the back of the car while Santo lays Zoe across the seat, her head resting on my lap. "She'll be okay, Marcel," he says.

"I know," I tell him.

She has to be. I can't imagine a life where she isn't. I have a whole new appreciation for my brother's grief. Not that I didn't before. But now, having experienced it, even for a short time... Well, the thought of Zoe being taken from me is not a reality I want to live in. Honestly, I don't know how the fuck he does it.

"If she's okay, then why isn't she waking up?" I ask the doctor, as he's stitching me back up. I made him look Zoe over first. He says she's fine. That she will wake up. That there aren't any serious injuries.

"She went through a traumatic event. Shock, anxiety, fear. It takes a toll on one's mind. She will wake up. And when she does, she will need help. I'd suggest getting her to see someone," Doc says.

I nod my head but don't say anything else. I have no idea how this is going to affect Zoe. She's already dealing with PTSD. I will do whatever I have to do to help her through it, though.

Doc packs up his shit, and a few seconds later, Gio and Santo follow him out. I refuse to leave Zoe, which is why we're in my room. She's in my bed. She looks peaceful, like she's sleeping.

"She's tough. She will get through this," Izzy says.

I look from her to Mikhail. "Do you think her panic attacks will get worse? More frequent?"

"I don't know. They're not as bad as they were

when we first found her. And this incident, it was bad, but nothing like what happened to her before," Izzy tells me.

I know she wasn't abused sexually, not this time at least, but she was locked in a room with a psychopath. And she saw her friend killed. "I'll do whatever she needs," I tell them.

"As will we," Izzy replies.

Mikhail's phone rings. He pulls it out from the front of his suit jacket before eyeing his wife. "It's Kon."

"Wait." I hold up a hand to stop him from answering. "Ask him where the fuck he was."

"What?"

"You heard me. Ask the fucker where he was. For the last few weeks, he's been following Zoe around with Ivan. Every day but today. Ask him why."

Mikhail nods his head, then leaves the room to take the call.

"You know, he likes you," Izzy says while glancing in my direction.

I snort. "I doubt that."

"Yeah, *like* is probably too strong. He respects you," she clarifies. "But she loves you, which makes us family."

"I love her." I stare at Zoe. Willing her to wake up.

Mikhail walks back into the room. "I need to pay Ivan's family a visit," he tells Izzy.

"Okay, I'll wait here," she says.

"Your father is blowing up my phone. Call him. The kids are fine, but he's not happy about being left with babysitting duties."

"Okay. I'll call him." Izzy leans in and kisses her husband. And I'm left to feel like I'm watching a very domesticated side of the Russian Pakhan that not many see.

"Let me know when she wakes up," Mikhail says before walking out again.

"I'm going to leave you to rest. You should try to get some sleep. When she wakes up, she'll need you more than she needs me," Izzy tells me.

Nodding at her in acknowledgement, I take hold of Zoe's hand and entwine our fingers together. I don't ever want to let go of her again. I'm already working on how I can get her to move in with me. Either here or maybe we'll get our own place. Just her and me. Like I told Gio I wanted to do.

Gabe bought a house, for him and his girl. Although Daisy is still here. She won't move into it without him. Maybe I'll get Eloise to find me a house in this neighbourhood too.

My big brother already tried to tell me it wasn't an option, and he lost his shit when he found out Gabe was planning on moving out. The guy is a control freak, and when we're not all under the same room, he can't keep as close an eye on us. He has this need to protect us.

I think it's time to move on, though.

I let my eyes close. Picturing our future. Mine and Zoe's. We'll have our own house, a dog, and eventually some kids running around too. I will spend every day of the rest of my life making sure she knows she's loved. Wholly and completely loved.

I'll chase her monsters away. I will fight her demons with her. We're going to get past this. It's going to take a while and it's not going to be easy. But we will come out the other end—that much I know for sure.

Chapter Thirty-Four

Whispered voices break through my unconsciousness. Waking me up. I open my eyes to see a sleeping Marcel right next to me.

Am I dreaming? Or is this heaven?

I glance around as recognition sinks in. I'm in

Marcel's room. Which means this can't be heaven. Because surely I'd be in a better designed room if it were.

Those same whispered voices have me stilling. I turn my head and see Izzy and Mikhail standing in the corner. Something I never thought I'd wake up to while sprawled out in Marcel's bed.

Marcel's bed. My head snaps back to him. He's here. But I saw him... I saw him on the ground with all the blood pooling around him. My eyes run up and down his torso. There's a huge bandage that covers half of his abdomen. He's not dead.

"Zoe? You're awake. Thank God!" Izzy takes a step closer to me.

I turn back to face her. She's standing right next to the bed now. "What happened?" I ask her.

"You passed out. Marcel insisted on bringing you here," she explains.

I look back at the man in question. He's still asleep. His hand is firmly clasping mine. I can't be here. Why would he bring me here?

"Izzy, I want to go home," I tell her. A stray tear escaping. I know what I have to do. I'm not going to like doing it, but I can't stay.

"Um, okay. Are you sure, Zoe?" she asks me.

I nod my head, not taking my eyes off Marcel. "I

have to," I whisper. He's alive, but for how much longer? I can't do this. I can't do love. The heartbreak is just too much.

It's easier if I break my own heart now. It has to be. I can't be the reason Marcel takes his last breath. I can't watch him die. I don't want to know that kind of pain again.

"Okay, give me a minute," Izzy says.

I nod but I don't take my eyes off Marcel. Then, untangling my fingers from his, I slowly slide out of the bed, trying not to wake him. Mikhail is standing at the doorway with a strange look on his face. He doesn't say anything, though. He simply takes my hand and leads me downstairs.

"Going somewhere?" Vin asks when I reach the lower landing.

"I..." I don't know what to say. "I have to go home."

He dips his head in acknowledgement more than agreement, if his next words are anything to go by. "You know he's not going to like waking up and finding you gone. Again."

"But he'll be alive to not like it," I remind him. "I'm sorry."

Vin continues up the stairs while calling out over a shoulder, "See you later, Zoe."

"Take me home. Please," I plead with Mikhail. If I don't do this now, I might not get the courage to do it at all.

"Let's go," he says, leading me towards the front door, where Izzy is talking to Marcel's brother.

Gio looks at me with... pity. I know how close Marcel and his brothers are. None of them are going to be okay with me walking out on him, like Vin said... *again.* I'm not okay with it either. I hate that I'm doing this. I just don't know any other way to protect myself and him.

"It's going to be okay," Izzy tells me. Wrapping her arm around my shoulder, she pulls me against her chest.

"Call if you need anything, Zoe," Gio grunts before walking away.

As soon as I walk into my house, I head straight for the shower. I stay under the spray of the hot water until my skin is red raw and I'm out of tears. Dressing in a pair of sweats and a hoodie, not thinking about the fact that said hoodie is Marcel's, I walk out to find Izzy and Mikhail in the kitchen.

"Where are the kids?" I ask, noticing how quiet the house is.

"My parents took them to the zoo," Izzy says. "Come sit down. You need to eat."

"I'm not hungry," I tell her.

"And I wasn't asking. Sit down," she says more firmly—in her mom tone—before placing a plate with a sandwich on the counter.

I lower my butt to the stool and glare at the plate. I wasn't lying. I'm really not hungry. All I want to do is go up to my bed, cover myself in the blankets, and forget the world exists.

"You know I'll go along with whatever you want. And, personally, I don't like the guy. But..." Mikhail says, picking up half of the sandwich from my plate and holding it out to me. I take it from him. "He loves you and he's not going to just let you walk away without a fight."

"He might." This is the second time I've walked out on him without an explanation. How much fight does one person have?

Mikhail's phone rings and he answers it, carrying out a conversation in his native tongue until the last sentence. "Let him in," he says while looking at me.

I shake my head. "I can't see him." I get up from the stool.

"You have to talk to him. If you want him to leave you alone, you can either convince him to do it with your words or I can make him disappear." Mikhail shrugs before adding, "Permanently." Just in case I didn't get his message loud and freaking clear.

"I'll talk to him." I sigh. "Just give me a minute." I walk up the stairs at the back of the house. I need to prepare myself to see him. I need to be able to look at him without crumbling, and I don't think I can do that just yet.

I walk back down when I hear Izzy and Mikhail leave the kitchen. I know it isn't right. But I just can't do this right now. I can't face him.

My own heart? I can break it. His? It'll be harder to see the hurt in his eyes. I open the back door and take one step on to the deck before a deep voice has me jumping on the spot.

"Sneaking out?"

"Santo, what the hell! You scared the crap out of me," I tell Marcel's brother.

"Sorry," he says. "Where are you going?"

"Why are you snooping around my backyard?"

"I came with Marcel. He used the front door. I

figured I'd come check out the back." He shrugs. "Where were you planning on hiding?"

"I wasn't," I lie.

"You were, but you should know, he'd probably sniff you out like one of those search dogs. He's not going to give up just because you run," Santo says.

"You were right," I tell him.

"I'm usually not, but what was I right about?" He chuckles.

"Love," I say. "It's only going to destroy us. There's no such thing as happily ever after. Love is a disaster waiting to happen."

"I was wrong." He shakes his head. "If you have love, Zoe, then hold on to it for as long as you can."

"I thought he was dead," I whisper. "I wanted to die too." Again, I don't know why I'm opening up to him.

"But he's not, and neither are you."

"It hurt. I can't do that." I lower myself onto the bench seat that faces out towards the garden.

"It does hurt, but that doesn't mean the days where you have each other aren't worth it. The days where you're beyond happy. That's an experience you shouldn't rob yourself of." Santo sits beside me.

"I don't think I can do it. It's my fault he got hurt. I can't be the reason he dies," I admit.

"There is no better reason to die than love, Zoe. Think about it. Are you really going to be okay if he chooses to move on? Marries some other woman and has that life that you two should be living together?"

I don't like the thought of Marcel with another woman. Not one bit. But I also don't like the thought of him being hurt. Or worse... killed. Because of me.

Chapter Thirty-Five

"**W**here the fuck is she?" As much as I try to keep my voice calm, low, I fail. My words come out harsh and loud. But can you blame me? I fucking woke up to my girlfriend missing from my bed, where I'd fallen asleep next to her.

I'm fucking fuming. How dare she just up and

leave like that. No note, no discussion, just... gone. Well, fuck that. If Zoe wants to put distance between us, she's going to have to try harder than just running back to her house. I'm not letting her go. Ever.

I don't care how hard she pushes. I will just push back harder. She can build all the walls she wants, because I'll knock them down. Leaving nothing but rubble where they once stood.

I will not let her break us, because I know she's it for me. If I don't have her, I don't want anyone. I don't want to breathe without her being mine.

"She will be down in a minute. She knows you're here," Izzy says.

She knows I'm here. I look up the stairs but my gut tells me she's not up there. Walking past both Mikhail and Izzy, I head through the house to the back door. I slide it open and pause on the threshold when I see Zoe sitting next to Santo on the bench seat.

Their backs are to me, but I know by the stiffening of Zoe's spine she heard me open the door. Santo pushes to his feet and turns around, making eye contact with me. He gives a slight nod before walking to the side of the house and disappearing around the corner.

For a moment, I don't move. Almost too afraid.

Worried that if I do, Zoe is going to either take off running or shut down on me completely. When she doesn't acknowledge my presence, I walk over and claim the spot Santo vacated.

Zoe's gaze is fixed on something in the backyard. Even when I turn to look at her, she doesn't move. "What did I do wrong?" I ask. Because right now, I have no fucking idea why she left and even less of a clue how to fix this.

"Nothing." Zoe's response is barely a whisper.

"Then why'd you leave?" This question has her turning to me, tears running down her cheeks. I reach up and wipe them away with my thumbs. "Don't cry. I'm sorry. Whatever it is, we can work it out, Zoe."

She shakes her head. "I thought you were dead."

"I'm very much not dead, babe." I smile at her, hoping to ease some of her sadness, her pain.

"That's not the point. I thought you were dead and I wanted... I wanted to die too. I didn't want to live anymore. I didn't fight. I just waited to die," she says.

My heart stops, and my mouth goes dry. "The thought of you dying breaks me, Zoe. Don't go doing that. Always fucking fight for yourself. Even if I'm not here anymore, I want you to live. I want you to live a long, full, happy life."

"I don't want to feel like that again, Marcel. I can't," she tells me.

"Babe, we can't live our lives scared of all the *what ifs*. If you do that, you miss out on all the good things that could be as well."

"I've never felt so much pain before in my life. You have taken my heart, Marcel, and it shattered. I'm not sure it can heal from that kind of breakage."

"I know that you're scared. I get it. When I found out you were... gone, I was fucking petrified I'd never see you again. I get it. I love you."

"I know," she says. "But I don't think I can love you anymore, Marcel."

Her words knock the wind out of me. I don't let her see that. She needs me to be the strong one. "That's okay. I can love myself enough for both of us," I tell her. "This isn't the end of our story, Zoe. This is just the first act. We have so much more coming."

"You don't get it. We need to end this before it's too late. I can't do this. I can't feel like that again. I won't." She stands up from the bench. Her voice rises with each breath she takes. Each word she sends my way.

Good, let her get angry. Anger is a feeling I can handle. It's far easier to see her angry than it is to see her fucking cry.

"No, you don't get it. There is no ending to this, Zoe. You and me, we're not fucking breakable. You got hurt. I'm sorry for that, but you are not the only person in this relationship. I'm right here too, and I get a choice. My choice is you, always you." I stand and take three steps, closing the gap between us. "Try your best to push me away, Zoe. I'm not going anywhere."

"No. We can't keep doing this. It's going to end badly. There's no such thing as happily ever after, not for us." She shoves at my chest.

I don't budge. "We have the chance to make our own happily ever after, Zoe. I'm not letting that go."

"I. Don't. Want. You. Here!" she yells out, landing her fists on my chest with a little more force.

Still, I don't move. But something crosses over Zoe's face. She stops, takes two steps backwards, and her eyes widen. She's scared.

"Yes you do," I tell her. "You can hit me all you like, Zoe. Fuck, shoot me if you have to. I'm not going anywhere."

"I'm sorry," she whispers.

"You know I'm not that guy. I will never raise a

hand to you. I will never hurt you." I step closer to her. "I don't fucking like seeing you scared of me," I say while wrapping my arms around her back. Then I pull her against my chest.

"I know you're not that guy. But I shouldn't have hit you either. I'm sorry. I'm so sorry," she repeats.

"You have nothing to be sorry about." I kiss the top of her head.

"I'm ruining everything. I don't know what to do anymore."

I can feel her tears soaking through my shirt. "It's okay, babe."

"It's not," she says.

"Zoe, whatever happens, it's you and me. We will find our way. I promise."

"I'm a mess, Marcel. You don't deserve to be stuck with someone like me."

"I'm not going anywhere. I'm right here. I'm here for all of it. The messy parts and the clean parts. I want them all. As long as I have you, I don't care what else happens," I tell her. "I love you, Zoe."

"I love you too much. It scares the crap out of me," she says.

"Well, we can be scared together. We can be happy together, sad together. Whatever we're feeling, we're doing it together."

She sighs, shaking her head while peering up at me through her damp lashes. "Why are you so perfect?"

"I'm far from perfect, babe. But for you, I'll never stop trying to be everything you need and want."

"You are so much more than that already. I'm sorry I ran... again."

"It's okay. I'll find you and bring you back every time," I tell her.

"What do we do now?" she asks.

"Now? You marry me. You let me have you for the rest of our lives."

"Okay," she says.

I blink down at her. That seemed way too easy. "Okay?" I repeat, questioning if she's really agreeing to my impromptu proposal right now.

"Yes. I'll marry you. Not that you actually asked the question. But my answer is yes."

"Holy shit. Yes? Shit. Babe, I'm going to make you the happiest wife in the world. I'm going to give you that happily ever after." I lean down and claim her lips, doing my best to express everything I'm feeling with this kiss. Showing her that my love will never falter.

She and I, we are one and the same. There isn't one without the other.

335

Epilogue

Fifteen months later

Have you ever waited for what seems like a lifetime for something? That's what today is for me. The day I've been waiting for. The day I become Mrs Marcello De Bellis. Of course, it was my choice to wait. Marcel would have married me the day he proposed if I'd let him.

Knowing how important his brothers are to him, though, I wanted to wait until he could have all four of them here with us. I'm glad I did too. Seeing the bond between the five De Bellis brothers, especially since Gabe's release, is unlike anything I've ever seen. I've never had siblings—the Petrov kids always looked at me as more of an aunt than a sister—but now I have four brothers and two sisters.

Eloise and I have become really close over the last year and a half. Considering how our first meeting went, it could have been so different. Daisy disappeared for a year while Gabe was away. No one knew where she was—well, no one but Vin, who decided to keep that titbit of information to himself. Along with the fact that she had a child. Luciano, a beautiful six-month-old baby boy. Since they learned of his existence, everyone has been doting on the newest De Bellis arrival. It won't be too long until Luciano has a cousin either. Eloise is ready to burst any day now.

I was wrong when I tried to run from what Marcel and have. Over the past year and a half, he's proven that we can have our happily ever after. That even though life can take unexpected turns, the one constant is our love for each other. And nothing will ever change that. It's unbreakable.

The door to the room opens and I turn around to find Mikhail—in a tux, mind you—waiting for me. "You know, if you're having second thoughts, I can get you out of here without anyone noticing," he says.

I laugh. "I'm not." I asked Mikhail to give me away during the planning process of the wedding.

He looked at me with confusion and said, "You think I'm going to let some other motherfucker walk you down the aisle?"

I took that as his way of saying yes.

The thought of asking anyone else was never there. Mikhail is the only father figure I have. He treats me with the same love and protection as his biological children. Although the events that led me to being in Mikhail and Izzy's life were horrific, and personally I'd do anything to erase them from my memory, I wouldn't want to erase Izzy or Mikhail. Their families or how they've become mine.

There was a moment after I was kidnapped that I thought his view of me might change. One of his best man died trying to protect me, and the other... Kon, the one who was supposed to be there with Ivan...

Well, Mikhail killed him for shirking his guard duties. It turned out he was with his girlfriend. Which was another strike against the rules Mikhail has for his men. Irina was a stripper at one of their clubs here before she quit and disappeared for a while. The men are not supposed to engage with the girls. Ever. According to Mikhail, they can't protect them properly if they're too busy trying to get into their pants.

"Okay, well, I guess it's time," he says, holding out his arm. I link my arm with his as Mikhail stares down at me. "Even though you are becoming a De Bellis today, you will always be a Petrov. Don't forget that," he says.

"Thank you." Tears prick my eyes. "If you make me cry and ruin my makeup, I think Izzy might stab you though." I laugh.

Mikhail lifts one shoulder. "Wouldn't be the first time." He smirks.

"Let's do this." I look at the double doors we're about to walk through and can't help but think it's symbolic. Like opening the doors to something new. Our story hasn't ended, as Marcel likes to tell me. It's only just beginning, and today is the start of the best chapter yet.

Zoe never fails to take my breath away. But right now? As she walks down the aisle towards me in a white dress, she's fucking stunning. I'm overcome with emotion watching her. All of my brothers are sitting in the front pew. Zoe and I decided not to have a wedding party, wanting to be the only ones on the altar.

When she reaches me, Mikhail holds on to her hand. I know he wants to pick her up and run. He's not a fan of Zoe growing up and getting married. I get it. I'd do anything to protect her too.

When he finally releases her, he turns to me. "If you ever break her heart, I'll make sure you regret the day you were born."

I nod my head. I'm not worried about his threats. It's not the first time I've heard him threaten me; it's probably not going to be the last either. I can handle it. Besides, I'm never going to break this girl's heart.

"You look beautiful," I tell her as I take hold of her hands.

"Thank you." She smiles.

The priest starts the ceremony, and I gotta be honest. I don't hear much of what he says. I'm too lost in Zoe's eyes to notice.

That's until she squeezes my hands and whispers, "It's your turn."

"Right, sorry." I turn to the priest.

"You've prepared your own vows, Mr De Bellis?" he questions.

"Yes." I turn back to the woman I can't live without and clear my throat. "Zoe, you are everything and more than I could ever have dreamt up in a partner. That's what you are. My partner, my best friend, my soul mate. I vow to love you through the good times and bad. Through all the healthy times, because I'm never letting you get sick. I promise to love you the way you deserve to be loved. I promise to always support your dreams, to be your strength when you don't have any, to be your light in the darker times. I promise to love you wholly and completely always."

The priest looks from me to Zoe. "Miss Petrov, have you prepared your own vows?"

"Yes." Zoe doesn't take her eyes off mine. "Marcello, I don't think Disney could dream up a better Prince Charming than you. You are my very own saviour, my best friend. I couldn't think of a better person to grow old with than you. I promise to always fight for us. I promise to put you above all else. To love you. To be your number one cheerleader, always and forever. I promise to fully embrace this crazy thing called life with you, to savour each chapter until the very end. I love you."

After we exchange our vows, the priest says the words I've been waiting a fucking long time to hear. "You may kiss your bride."

I don't wait for him to finish his sentence. My lips are on Zoe's within a heartbeat. Picking my wife up off the ground, I spin her around. "I love you, Mrs De Bellis," I whisper against her lips before claiming them again.

Are you dying to know what happened when Mikhail and Izzy found Zoe all those years ago? Continue reading for a two chapter sneak peak of The Legacy of Valentino Duet.

Legacy of Valentino Duet - Sample

Mikhail

Have you ever walked in on something you wished you could unsee? That's what's happening to me right fucking now. I've seen a lot of messed-up shit in my life. Shit, I can stomach practically anything. But what I've just witnessed, what I've just walked into— yeah, I can't fucking unsee that.

This pathetic excuse for a human being was on

top of a girl, a fucking girl who can't be any older than fourteen. Her screams and pleas for help were the first thing I heard when I stepped inside the house. I pulled him off her, and when I noticed the blood between her legs, the angry welts all over her naked body—I saw fucking red. I lost it.

Paul untied the girl and wrapped a blanket around her shoulders. She's now sitting in the corner of the room, refusing to talk or look at anyone. I don't want to traumatize the kid any more than she has been. So I drag the fat fucker out of the bedroom. He's unconscious, and for what I want to do to him, I'm going to need the son of a bitch to wake the fuck up.

I can wait, though. I pull the cable ties out of my pocket and bind his hands behind his back and his feet together at the ankles. Leaving him hog-tied like the pig he is, I walk to the front door where I left the asshole from the trunk.

When I found this case on Isabella's website, it was as if the gods were handing me a gift on a silver platter. The guy who's about to find out what happens to men who rape innocent women and girls is a reasonably high-level IRA member. While the fucker who's being framed is another Irish bastard looking to climb the ranks.

The thing about the Stiletto Killer, they've been targeting made men from every organization all over the city. There isn't a syndicate around that won't want to seek revenge for their lost brothers. Even if those so-called brothers deserved everything that was handed to them.

Dragging the heavy fucker inside, I kick the door shut and leave him in the hall. He isn't waking up anytime soon with the amount of drugs I forced into his system. Then I position myself on the sofa and wait for my main event to come to. I don't want to start the show without him.

Paul exits the room a few seconds later, his face pale and his shoulders tense. He doesn't like the scene we walked into any more than I do. "She won't talk. What are we going to do with her?"

I have no fucking idea. I don't blame the girl for not talking. After what she's been through, I wouldn't want to talk to a pair of strange men who busted through the doors wielding guns either. Especially when it's obvious those men aren't cops.

My phone buzzes with a text before I can answer Paul. Pulling the device out of my pocket, I stare at the words on the screen.

Lex: Mrs. Petrov is on her way, boss. I

couldn't stop her. I'm driving though. Her parents are with the baby.

Fucking Isabella, I should have known she wouldn't let things lie. How the fuck did she find out where I was headed?

"Did Lex know where we were headed tonight?" I ask aloud.

"No, I was going to plug the address into the GPS when you told him to go inside," Paul says. "Why?"

"Isabella is on her way here," I groan.

Paul smiles. "Your wife never ceases to impress me, boss."

"Yeah, me too," I say, unsure if I should be more proud or annoyed at the moment.

"It could be a good thing. I mean, that girl in there..." He points to the room he just exited. "...needs a woman to talk to. She ain't gonna trust us. We can't help her the way Izzy can." Most of my men refer to my wife as *Mrs. Petrov*. Paul is the only one who uses her shortened name.

"Yeah, you're probably right," I say.

"I usually am." Paul shrugs before dropping down next to me on the sofa.

If Isabella just left the house, that means she's going to be here in around twenty minutes. By then, the show will be well on its way. So Paul and I sit in silence until the fat Irish fucker finally decides to come to. He pulls at his wrists while his legs buck on the ground.

"There really is no point trying. You won't get out of those ties. Besides, if I need 'em, I have plenty more where they came from," I tell him. Pushing to my feet, I close the distance between us. His face is already bruised from where my fist connected with it earlier—the one punch that knocked him out cold.

"Fuck you. You're fucking dead," he spits.

"Am I though? Seems to me like I'm here in the flesh, living and breathing," I say, patting my hands down my chest. "You, on the other hand? I'd say you're about to meet your maker, but we know there is only one place scum like you go. Straight to the pits of hell."

"I'm going to skin you alive," he threatens.

"I'm right here. What are you waiting for?" I ask, holding my arms out wide. "Oh, that's right, your hands are a *wee* bit tied right now." I laugh.

"That slut wanted it," he tries to argue.

"Yeah, you see, it didn't really sound that way to me." I kick my booted foot at his ribs, smiling when I hear the crack of bones. He screams like a fucking banshee. "Paul, muzzle it. I don't want to hear that shit."

Paul draws a pocket square from his jacket and then pulls a roll of duct tape out of the bag he had at the ready. I watch as he shoves the fabric in the guy's mouth and then tears off a piece of tape, securing it over the bastard's lips.

"That should do it," Paul says.

I look at my watch. I probably have about five minutes before Isabella shows up guns blazing. I bend down and take the knife from my ankle. She liked to focus her attention on certain parts of her target's bodies. I need to make sure I stab the exact same spots to make this appear as though it's a legit Stiletto Killer job.

I bring my knife to his face first and draw a line from just under his right eye to his chin, cutting only skin deep. I then repeat the process under his left eye. Stepping back, I take in my handiwork, noticing how the tiny droplets of blood drip down from his jaw. They look like tears, bloody tears.

Is this why Isabella does it? To represent the tears of the countless women and children these assholes abuse. Sometimes I wish I could climb inside my wife's brain and read her thoughts.

The front door swings open with a bang and I

hear the telltale click-clack of a pair of heels heading towards me. Stepping around the fucker who is making god-awful grunts and groans through his makeshift gag, I meet Isabella halfway across the room. Where I take hold of the back of her head, tilt her face upwards, and slam my lips onto hers, pushing my tongue past the seam of her closed mouth. She opens on a moan that I greedily swallow. I escape into that kiss, into being connected to Isabella like this is fucking everything. I can't get enough of the feeling she gives me.

Pulling away slightly, I growl, "What the fuck are you doing here, kotyonok?"

"The same thing you're doing here. What on earth were you thinking?" she says, shoving at my chest. I take a step back because I want to, not because she's forcing me.

"I was thinking I was clearing my wife's name so she can carry on living her life to the fullest," I tell her.

"You should have told me you had some cooked-up idea." She steps around me, examining the room, with barely a glance at the two bodies on the floor. "What exactly is the plan here?" she asks.

"The plan is to mimic one of the murders, spread this fucker's prints everywhere, and wait for the dumb fucks to connect the dots." I cross my arms over my chest and watch her.

She looks at both men. And then smiles. "That's actually not as stupid as it sounds."

"Gee, thanks for the vote of confidence," I huff.

"Ah, boss?" Paul grabs my attention. He nods his head towards the bedroom door where the girl is still seated. She hasn't moved, hasn't made a peep either.

I give him a nod and turn back to my wife. "Isabella, when we got here, he wasn't alone," I tell her.

"Okay?"

"There's a girl in the room. She's... distraught, for lack of a better word, and won't talk to either of us. We had to pull him off her." I pause until Isabella catches my meaning.

She doesn't say anything as she steps up to the guy on the floor and kicks a pointy-toed shoe at his groin. "Filthy fucking bastard," she hisses, then peers back up at me. "Don't touch him. I'm going to talk to her." Isabella disappears into the room, and like a pup anticipating its next command, I wait for my wife to return.

Legacy of Valentino Duet - Sample

I can't believe the depths that Mikhail is willing to go to in order to get me out of a mess I created long before I met him. Don't get me wrong, I'm still pissed as hell that he hacked into my website and didn't tell me what he was planning to do.

Then again, at the same time, I think this is probably the most romantic thing anyone has ever done for me. I know... murder and shit shouldn't be romantic, but it's the gesture behind the blood and gore that had me practically swooning at my husband's feet. I probably need therapy—though that's not going to be something I'm seeking soon. Because when I married Mikhail, I accepted all parts of him, just as he did with me. We are two twisted souls who found each other against every possible odd that wasn't in our favor.

When I walk into the room, I have to count to ten to stop myself from going back out there and unleashing all hell on the fucking asshole who is currently squirming around the floor. The girl is sitting in the corner, her knees drawn up to her chest and a blanket wrapped around her shoulders. For a moment, I have a flashback of my Zia Lola on the floor of her bedroom in this exact same position. I quickly shake that image away and focus on the task at hand.

This girl can't be older than fifteen. She's tiny, fragile, and when she looks up at me, all I see in her eyes is fear. It's a good thing, though, because at least her gaze isn't blank yet. That means she's still fighting. She hasn't taken herself someplace else, leaving behind an empty shell.

I kneel down in front of her. "Hi, my name is

Isabella. My friends call me Izzy," I tell her. "What's your name?"

She peers up at me with tears streaming down her face. "Are you going to tell them?" she asks.

"Tell who?"

"The men who sold me to him? I don't want to go back. Please don't send me back," she begs, and I can hear the desperation in her voice.

"I'm never going to let you go back. Okay? I'm here to help you," I assure her, then repeat my question. "What's your name?"

"Zoe. My name is Zoe," she says.

"It's nice to meet you, Zoe." I smile, keeping my hands on my knees. I don't want her to shy away and I know the last thing she wants right now is to be touched. "How old are you, Zoe?"

"Seventeen."

"Where are your parents? Do you live near here?" I continue to probe her for information while trying to ensure I don't come off too demanding.

"I..." She shakes her head. "My dad gave me to those men," she says.

I want to pick this girl up and wrap her in my arms. I can't believe a parent—any parent—would do such a thing to their own child. I'm going to find out who her father is and add him to the top of my hit list. Fucking asshole.

"It's okay. I'm going to get you out of here. I'm going to take you home with me and then we can figure things out from there, okay?" Zoe doesn't say anything, but she does nod her head, so I continue. "I need you to do me a favor, Zoe. I need you to cover your ears. Don't come out of this room until I come back to get you. Think you can do that for me?"

"Where are you going? Please don't leave me here. Don't leave me with them." She starts panicking.

"I'm not leaving. I'm just going to be in the living room. I need to make sure that the man who did this to you can't ever do it again to anyone else," I tell her.

"Please, don't leave me." She's crying now, fresh tears streaking her dirt-riddled skin.

"I promise I'm not leaving you." I glance behind me to the door. "I have a friend out there. Lex. I can get him to wait with you if you don't want to be alone." Her eyes widen, and terror overtakes her once more. Which was exactly what I feared happening. I don't blame her for not wanting to be around men, but I don't have many options at the moment. I decide to change tact. "It's okay. You know what? I'm going to bring you home now. Come on." I hold out my hand for her to take.

"What about the man?" she asks. "He'll find me again."

"No, he won't. My husband is out there and he'll make sure he's gone."

"Your husband?"

"My husband is the one who found you. Mikhail."

Zoe nods again, then she places the palm of her hand in mine. She's nothing but skin and bone under the blanket. How fucking long has she been enduring this nightmare?

Maybe I should call Zio James and have him sit down and speak with her. He's a trained therapist and an expert in this kind of trauma. But that would mean letting his wife, my Zio Lola, know what's been going on, and I don't want to take her back to her own nightmare—the one she endured when she lived in captivity for ten years.

I don't stop moving when we make it to the living room. I lead Zoe right down the hallway. I don't want her to witness the scene that's playing out in there. "Mikhail," I call through the house and wait for him to follow me. He looks from Zoe to me. "I'm taking her home. I need you to finish what you started here."

"Home?" he questions.

"Our place. She doesn't have anywhere to go. I'll explain later." I lean up and kiss his lips quickly before walking out the door with Zoe in tow.

By the time we get to the car, Lex is running to catch up with me. Zoe's body completely freezes as he approaches us. "I'm driving, but we have to take the SUV. It's just down the road."

"Okay, well, we'll wait here while you go and get it," I tell him. Lex turns around, and within two minutes, he's pulling up next to the curb. I open the passenger door and wait for Zoe to get inside. "It's okay. Trust me. He's one of the good ones," I assure her. Her hand strangles mine as she climbs into the back seat of the car. I follow after her and shut the door.

The ride home is quiet. I can tell Zoe isn't sure what to think about all that's happening. I have so many questions I want to ask her, but now isn't the time. I'm the first to break the silence. "Lex, can you ask the doctor to meet us at the house?"

"Sure thing, Mrs. Petrov," he says.

"Thank you."

When we arrive home, I ask Lex to send my mom up to the guest room directly next to mine before leading Zoe there myself. Her eyes are wide as she takes in the house.

"This is where you live?" Her voice is filled with awe.

"Uh-huh, I haven't lived here long though. This is my husband's place. I just moved in."

"Is he... never mind." She shakes her head.

"Is he what? You can ask me anything, Zoe. It's okay," I urge her to continue.

"Is he going to send me back?"

"No, he would never do such a thing, and if he tried—not that he would—I'd kill him," I tell her.

"I don't want to be a bother," she says, seemingly unaffected by my threats of murder, which tells me more than I wish it did.

"You are not a bother."

"Izzy, what's going on?" my mom questions me the moment she enters the room.

"Where's Mabilia?"

"With your father. He's been hogging her all night." She pouts.

"Mama, this is Zoe. We need to find her some clothes, help her shower," I say. "Do you want a shower, Zoe?"

The girl nods her head.

"Okay, the bathroom is right through here. There are towels and everything you should need in there. You go ahead. I'm going to find you something to wear," I tell her.

After Zoe walks into the bathroom, I ask my mom to wait in the bedroom while I run to my closet to find a shirt and some comfy pajama pants. They're going to be too big for her, but at least they have a drawstring she can tighten. I place the clothes on the bed and sit down. The sound of the shower running carries through the bathroom door, which was left slightly ajar.

"What's going on?" Mom repeats.

"Mikhail went to recreate one of my scenes. When he got there, he found the guy assaulting her." I gesture to the bathroom. "She doesn't have anywhere to go. Her father sold her to traffickers, Mama. What kind of person would do that?" I know the answer, though. Because I know firsthand what kind of person would do that. My biological father was a trafficker himself, a sick fuck who got off on hurting children and women.

"So, she can stay with us. We have room," Mom offers.

"I think I'm going to let her stay here. I need to help her, Mama."

My mom brushes a hand down the side of my face, sweeping my hair aside. "Okay, baby, what do you want me to do? How can I help?"

"I don't know," I say.

A loud wail comes from the bathroom, and I bolt inside to find Zoe rocking back and forth on the shower floor. Stepping into the stall, I wrap my arms around her and pull her into my chest.

"Shh, it's okay. It's going to be okay. I promise. I have you. I'm not going to let anyone hurt you again." I sit there and hold her until the water goes cold. Then I push to my feet, bringing Zoe with me, and pull a huge fluffy towel from the rack. I ensure she's covered before grabbing one for myself too.

Also by kylie Kent

The Merge Series

Merged With Him (Zac and Alyssa's Story)

Fused With Him (Bray and Reilly's Story)

Entwined With Him (Dean and Ella's Story)

2nd Generation Merge Series

Ignited by Him (Ash and Breanna's Story)

An Entangled Christmas: A Merge Series Christmas Novel (Alex and Lily's Story)

Chased By him (Chase & Hope's Story)

Tethered To Him (Noah & Ava's Story)

Seattle Soulmates

Her List (Amalia and Axel Williamson)

McKinley's Obsession Duet

Josh and Emily's Story

Ruining Her

Ruining Him

Sick Love Duet

Unhinged Desires (Dominic McKinley and Lucy Christianson)

Certifiable Attraction (Dominic McKinley and Lucy Christianson)

The Valentino Empire

Devilish King (Holly and Theo's story)

Unassuming Queen (Holly and Theo's story)

United Reign (Holly and Theo's story)

Brutal Princess (Neo and Angelica's Story)

Reclaiming Lola (Lola and Dr James)

Sons of Valentino Series

Relentless Devil (Theo & Maddie's story)

Merciless Devil (Matteo & Savannah's story)

Soulless Devil (Romeo & Livvy's Story)

Reckless Devil (Luca & Katerina's Story)

A Valentino Reunion (The entire Valentino Family)

The Tempter Series

Following His Rules (Xavier & Shardonnay)

Following His Orders (Nathan &Bentley)

Following His Commands (Alistar & Dani)

Legacy of Valentino

Remorseless Devilette (Izzy and Mikhail)

Vengeful Devilette (Izzy and Mikhail)

Vancouver Knights Series

Break Out (Liam and Aliyah)

Know The Score (Grayson and Kathryn)

Light It Up Red (Travis and Liliana Valentino)

Puck Blocked (Luke and Montana)

De Bellis Crime Family

A Sinner's Promise (Gio and Eloise)

A Sinner's Lies (Gabe & Daisy)

A Sinner's Virtue (Marcel & Zoe)

A Sinner's Saint (Vin & Cammi)

A Sinner's Truth (Santo & Aria)

Club Omerta

Are you a part of the Club?

Don't want to wait for the next book to be released to
the public?
Come and Club Omerta for an all access pass!

This includes:
• daily chapter reveals,
• first to see - everything, covers, teasers, blurbs
• Advanced reader copies of every book
• Bonus scenes from the characters you love!
• Video chats with me (Kylie Kent)
• and so much more

Click the link to be inducted to the club!!!
CLUB OMERTA

About the Author

About Kylie Kent

Kylie made the leap from kindergarten teacher to romance author, living out her dream to deliver sexy, always and forever romances. She loves a happily ever after story with tons of built-in steam.

She currently resides in Sydney, Australia and when she is not dreaming up the latest romance, she can be found spending time with her three children and her husband of twenty years, her very own real life instant-love.

Kylie loves to hear from her readers; you can reach her at: author.kylie.kent@gmail.com

Let's stay in touch, come and hang out in my readers group on Facebook, and follow me on instagram.

Made in United States
Troutdale, OR
05/28/2026

49559917R00206